THE
STOLEN
CITY

THE STOLEN CITY

TOM EGLINGTON

PICCADILLY PRESS • LONDON

For Ollie and Eddie

First published in Great Britain in 2010
by Piccadilly Press Ltd,
5 Castle Road, London NW1 8PR
www.piccadillypress.co.uk

A catalogue record for this book is available from the British Library

ISBN: 978 1 84812 075 4 (paperback)

1 3 5 7 9 10 8 6 4 2

Printed in the UK by CPI Bookmarque Ltd, Croydon, CR1 4PD
Cover design by Patrick Knowles
Cover illustrations by Mark Robinson

CHAPTER ONE

SMALL THINGS

It happened on the first day of the summer holidays.

Bethany Chase and her parents had started their day expecting a scenic train journey down to London in pleasant sunshine. It wasn't long, though, before they were dealing with delays, disruptions, overcrowded carriages and numerous queues. The weather became unbearably hot and stifling. And now they had arrived, Mr Chase insisted that they see the sights of London by taking a bus to Aunt Bess's house, even though Bethany and her mother were weighed down with an assortment of heavy bags that seemed to encourage almost everyone to barge into them. It didn't help that it was late afternoon and the bus was full of miserable-looking people returning home from work, or that Bethany and her parents had to stand up for the entire journey, barely able to glimpse the landmarks Mr Chase excitedly called out as they made their way through the city centre.

'Look, in the distance – Big Ben!' he said in an overly keen voice. 'Always looks smaller in real life, doesn't it? And the Houses of Parliament. Guy Fawkes tried to blow that up, you know.'

Bethany tried to smile with interest but deliberately edged away from her father, wondering if there were some slightly less embarrassing adults she could pretend were her parents for the duration of the trip. Her father couldn't have looked more like a tourist, having decided to wear a disastrous combination of brightly coloured shorts, stripy shirt and sunglasses. Her mother, meanwhile, had spent most of the day rummaging through her bags, double checking tickets and maps, and generally fussing over Bethany and Mr Chase. She was doing this now in a very loud, noticeable manner. After a short pause she thrust a bottle of water at her daughter. 'Drink? You need to keep hydrated, you know. How about a snack? I have crisps or fruit.'

'I'm fine,' Bethany replied sullenly, focusing all her attention on the book she had been trying to lose herself in for most of the day.

'I think that's Nelson's Column!' her father blurted out, rudely jabbing a finger at the window and nearly catching a passenger on the cheek.

'*Dad*,' Bethany hissed.

He barely noticed her embarrassment or the attention he was attracting from the other passengers as they peeked disapprovingly over their newspapers at him. At each stop, people surged on and off the bus so quickly that Bethany was jostled to and fro, narrowly avoiding being pushed over altogether.

'Well, this is nice,' her mother chirped pleasantly. 'It's like one of those bus tours.'

'Hmm, sort of,' Bethany replied, less enthusiastically. 'But one where you can't see anything or get a seat.'

'Cheeky.' Mrs Chase laughed, ruffling her daughter's hair.

Bethany had not wanted to leave Stagtree Knoll for the summer holidays. Whereas once she would have relished visiting a new city, now the idea filled her with dread, especially somewhere with so many old buildings. Bethany didn't like old buildings and avoided them at all costs.

It had been her parents' idea to come to London. They had decided to rent their house out as a holiday home and stay with Mr Chase's sister, Aunt Bess, for most of the summer. They made it sound as though it was exciting and adventurous, but Bethany knew the real reason. She had heard her parents talking one night when they'd thought she'd gone to bed, discussing the factory where her father worked, how the contracts were drying up, how there were rumours of closures, how he never had enough hours. She had overheard his plans to look for new jobs in London, with the possibility that they might move there. It made her anxious. She had only just got used to living in Stagtree

Knoll and didn't think she could deal with all the upheaval of moving somewhere new.

Bethany knew that wasn't the real reason she was feeling so tense today, though. She couldn't avoid the memories of last summer and the strange adventure she'd experienced. Or at least *thought* she'd experienced. After all, what she recollected was, by most people's standards, unbelievable. Who would believe that she had stepped over into the spirit realm and found herself trapped in a hotel for ghosts, spirits and non-material beings? Who would believe she had helped a giant trapped in a pit, or that she had met the ghosts of conjoined twins working as cleaning ladies, or made friends with a mischievous pooka? And who would believe that she had defeated the Jackomuss demon, a demon that threatened to destroy her parents and enslave many others under its sinister influence?

No one, that was who. That was why Bethany never talked about what had happened. That was why in the year that had followed those peculiar events she had become quiet and cautious. She worried what other people might think about her, or that they would laugh at her, and so she kept a distance between herself and other children, trying her best to forget. At school, she avoided making friends, instead concentrating on her schoolwork and losing herself in books. She became particularly interested in the supernatural and would read up on all sorts of paranormal events and folklores and myths, hoping to find clues that would either confirm or deny her own experiences. And when the other children at school had joked about her being boring, so what? Bethany had enjoyed enough excitement for one lifetime, thank you very much. She had fought a demon and survived. Now all she wanted was a quiet life.

Her mind filled with those thoughts now. She had done a good job of letting them fade from her memory in recent months, but something – the summer weather, the travelling – was causing them to stir again. She found herself picturing the Spellbound Hotel, running along its corridors in fear, her friend at her side. The image of Quinn popped into her head and it made her smile. She could see his wide and round face, his impossibly large grin and his quiff of pink hair . . .

And that was when it happened.

Bethany idly glanced out of the window of the bus as it came to a halt behind a long line of traffic and saw a face staring back at her. It was a very peculiar face, wide and round, with an impossibly large grin, a quiff of pink hair, a small lumpy nose and eyes that glinted with mischief.

'Quinn?' Bethany called out. A mixture of feelings welled up in her in that single moment: shock, happiness, disbelief. She uttered a startled noise somewhere between a laugh and a shriek, and stumbled backwards. A hand caught her and stopped her from tripping over entirely. Her book fell to the floor.

No, it can't be!

She was standing at the centre of a throng of adults, all

frowning at her. Someone handed her the book she had dropped. Bethany thanked them, then looked out of the window again, but Quinn's face had disappeared. In its place stood a bored-looking office worker leafing through a magazine as he waited for the lights to change. The bus pulled away.

It's hot, Bethany decided, *that's all*. Her head spun a little and she eagerly grabbed the water her mother offered to her a second time.

'Did you just call out to someone?' Mrs Chase asked, squinting out of the window.

'No, no. Just daydreaming,' Bethany said quickly. *Stupid*, she chided herself. *It couldn't have been Quinn, that would be impossible. It would mean . . .* But she didn't want to think about what that would mean. She didn't want to think about it at all.

The bus chugged on towards Hyde Park, with Mr Chase commenting loudly on Marble Arch. Bethany tried to concentrate on what he was saying but her mind teemed with all sorts of buried memories, wonderful and alarming, that were springing to the surface. There was the group of leprechauns that had infested the hotel, and the bizarre library of singing tongues, and the demon. She shivered as she pictured it. It was a foul thing that resembled a black flame, flickering, unnatural.

Pull yourself together, she told herself. *You have not just seen a spirit of mischief in central London.*

As the bus passed out of the city centre, Mr Chase ran out of historic sights to comment on and became gradually quieter.

Bethany's attention shifted to the busy neighbourhoods they passed through and all the different styles of houses. It was on such a large scale compared to the size of their village that she soon stopped dwelling on thoughts of the spirit realm. They finally reached their destination some twenty minutes later, stepping out on to a fairly ordinary main road of shops with streets of redbrick terraced houses leading off from it.

'Follow me, troops,' Mr Chase joked. He walked confidently down a nearby street. Mrs Chase waited patiently until he came back, blushing, and headed off in the other direction. 'I was looking at the map the wrong way round,' he explained.

'Of course, dear,' she said tactfully.

Bethany followed. 'So, why haven't I met Aunt Bess before?' she asked.

'She is a bit eccentric, your aunt,' her mother replied. 'She doesn't tend to stray far out of London. Or her house, come to think of it.'

'That's an exaggeration,' Mr Chase said defensively. 'She's very nice and you have met her, Bethany, but you were very small at the time. I know my sister may seem a little bit odd to some people,' he shot a warning look at Mrs Chase, 'but she is letting us stay for the summer, which is extremely generous. So please bear that in mind.'

Bethany nodded. They came to the end of the road and Mr Chase halted at a rusted gate. The house he had stopped by had been built a few feet off the end of a terraced row of houses, giving it an odd, detached appearance as if it was turning away from the other buildings. A tall, scruffy hedge occupied most of the front garden.

'Right, this is us,' he announced in an excited tone. He stepped through the gate and dropped his bags on the ground by the porch. There was a large front window and he peeked through the dusty pane for signs of life. Bethany and Mrs Chase peered round him. They could just make out a dingy, cluttered room with a sofa and bookshelves. A group of shapes rushed to the window and several sets of small green eyes glinted back at them. Mr Chase murmured uncertainly at the sight of them before pressing the doorbell. Almost at once the shrill bell set off an explosion of barks, miaows, squawks and howls, followed by a rush of tiny feet. This was punctuated a few moments later by a heavier set of footfalls and a stern female voice. 'Get down! Get down! No, Bernard. Down! No, Marjorie, get out from there. I said *down!*'

The Chases took a cautious step back as the door opened, fully expecting to be engulfed by a stampede of various animals. Instead, an exceedingly tall woman with bright orange lipstick appeared, managing to hold back a collection of excited pets jumping up behind her. She tried her best to grin in a welcoming manner. A marmalade cat broke free from her grasp and dashed out towards the road. 'Catch him!' Aunt Bess said in a strained voice.

Luckily, Mrs Chase clasped the animal by the collar before it made it out of the gate. Bethany and her parents were quickly ushered into the house and were soon being sniffed and pawed by a selection of very energetic dogs and curious cats. Above them, cages of colourful budgies twittered and fluttered.

'Sorry we're late,' Mr Chase said, pecking his sister on the cheek. 'Delays in Grantham.'

'Oh, not to worry. Come through. Come through,' Aunt Bess said in a jolly tone. She had a long thin face, which was very animated, with lots of bright turquoise mascara around her eyes and a head of bushy hair that bore an uncanny resemblance to the overgrown hedge in the front garden. 'It's been too long, it really has. And look at you, Bethany. You're practically touching the ceiling.'

Bethany smiled. There was something immediately likeable about her aunt. Her house was almost the opposite of the Chases': chaotic, cluttered and lively. Stacks of books littered the shelves, mixed in with an assortment of colourful ornaments and exotic pot plants. The cats had made a series of paths through this bric-a-brac which they briefly retreated to for safety as a scuffle broke out between the dogs.

'Thanks for having us, sis,' Mr Chase said over the yapping and mewling sounds. 'You're a lifesaver, you really are.'

'Nonsense. Anything to help out,' she replied, prising apart the two fighting terriers at her feet. 'Behave, Bernard. And you, Spike.'

'Yes, this is . . . lovely,' Mrs Chase said. She couldn't help noticing the thick balls of fur that had gathered around the edges of the room and tried her best to hide an expression of rising alarm. She quickly searched through her bag and produced a box of chocolates. 'These are just to say thank you.'

'Oh, you shouldn't have. It's really no bother having you.' Aunt Bess nudged an older brown Labrador out of the way, then stroked a plump tabby that seemed to be wheezing rather than purring. 'Now then, I'll let you unpack and then I'll bring out sandwiches and cakes. I expect you're famished, and it will be nice to catch up over a cup of tea. Bethany, you're in the room at the top of the stairs. It's quite snug, but hopefully you'll fit.' She showed Bethany to the foot of the stairs and pointed to the door directly at the top. 'You're in the big bedroom,' she told Bethany's parents. 'Up and along.'

Walking up the narrow staircase was an interesting and hazardous task, with the small herd of animals steadily moving in front of Bethany's every step. The cats and dogs wore the expressions of animals anticipating a treat or food, and seemed upset when Bethany closed the bedroom door on them. She found herself standing in an extremely small room that looked as if it was only ever used for storage. Boxes of all sizes were stacked up along the walls. A single bed had somehow been squeezed into the middle of this, looking suspiciously like it had been propped on top of a mass of old suitcases. Bethany slumped down on to the edge of the bed and dropped her bags to the floor. She peered through the tiny square window directly level with the top of the mattress and found herself looking into the window of the adjacent house. It looked much cleaner next door, she had to admit. And she imagined it must be quieter. The animals were making a racket in the hall, thumping and scrabbling and snuffling.

'Oh well,' she sighed, imagining the long summer ahead in this cramped little space. It could be worse, she thought. And at that she thought of the image of Quinn's smiling face and all the trouble that meeting him again could lead to.

Almost as soon as his name popped into her head, a peculiar thing happened. The nearest and tallest pile of boxes shuddered. Bethany sat bolt upright. She almost leaped backwards as the stack of boxes quivered a second time.

'Is someone there?' she asked without thinking. *Of course there couldn't be anyone there, there was barely enough space for her.*

Nevertheless, the boxes shook again as if reacting to her words, the top ones moving as if they were nodding. Bethany felt herself panic. She stood up with her back against the door and in a barely audible whisper asked, 'Quinn, is that you?'

The boxes shook furiously, then fell still. Something scuttled from under the bed. Bethany instinctively jumped out of the way, only to bang into an old fashioned trunk. Shocked, she looked around her feet and saw a black cat stepping from behind a fallen box. It had short sleek fur and a long tail that curled round in a way that reminded Bethany of a question mark. It peered up at her with intense orange eyes, slanted and almost luminous, that gave it a very eerie appearance.

'A cat,' she muttered at herself, and burst into a fit of giggles. Of course it was a cat, she thought. What else did she expect in this house? 'You're not supposed to be in here,' she told it.

The animal stared back at her with a great deal of interest and Bethany pulled open the door and shooed it out, then followed it downstairs, as she joined her parents and Aunt Bess. They were already gathered round a small oval table loaded with tea and plates of food.

'Help yourself,' Aunt Bess said, handing Bethany a mug of tea. 'Now there's egg and cress, tuna or cheese mayo. Or there's quiche. And have as many cupcakes as you want.'

The food all looked homely and attractive and, Bethany noticed, slightly hairy. Mr Chase was busy chomping through a sandwich, before gulping it down noisily with several slurps of tea.

'I must say, this makes a nice change. I'm not really used to having visitors,' Aunt Bess remarked, proffering the plate of cupcakes at Bethany and her mother.

'Well, we're just sorry we've not made it down sooner,' Mrs Chase said, plucking a cat hair from the icing on her cake.

'I like your house,' Bethany told her aunt. She had noticed lots of unusual paintings filling one wall. They were, predictably, pictures of animals but they had been done using lots of bright, lively colours. 'And all your animals. What's the black cat called?'

'Black cat?' Aunt Bess said. She brushed a Siamese off her lap as it made a lunge at the quiche.

'Yeah, it's got sort of funny orange eyes,' Bethany explained.

Her aunt looked perplexed and said in a surprised tone, 'No, I don't have any black cats. I've not had a black cat since Sylvester died a few years ago.'

'But it was just in my room. It's probably here somewhere.' Bethany scanned the mob of animals all looking up expectantly in the hope of being fed a scrap of food, but it wasn't there.

'Not to worry. It might be a stray that's come in through the catflap. Just put it out if you see it again.' Aunt Bess smiled, then coughed very suddenly and very loudly. 'Haaarkf ccurrrff cccurrff!' She dabbed the sides of her mouth with a napkin. 'Sorry, cat hair,' she explained, then quickly offered the plate of sandwiches to her guests again. 'Any more for any more?'

Bethany drifted off as Mr and Mrs Chase began talking about the details of their stay. She was thinking about the nervous feeling in her stomach and trying to tell herself that she definitely had not seen Quinn and that there was nothing unusual about the black cat. *This is going to be a completely normal summer*, she told herself. She surveyed the chaos of her aunt's house and felt a twinge of doubt. *Well, maybe not completely normal.*

CHAPTER TWO

CATS
AND CAKES

Most of the following few days were spent sightseeing and exploring parts of London. Mr Chase led the way in a determined, excited manner, with Bethany and her mother trailing after him. They were dragged into packed underground stations, through bustling markets, around echoing museums and inside vast shops, noise and activity swirling around them at every turn. Bethany had never seen so many people before and felt overwhelmed whenever she was carried along in a particularly large crowd, feeling as if she was caught in the current of a slow-moving river from which it was impossible to escape.

Mr Chase insisted on taking them round all the major landmarks he could find. He amused himself by getting

Mrs Chase to photograph him standing close to the lens so that he appeared to be a giant squashing Big Ben under his thumb, or preparing to take a bite out of St Paul's Cathedral, or making it look as if he was pushing Tower Bridge over. They both found this hilarious and kept thinking up new positions to try, bursting into loud giggling fits as they viewed the results. Bethany dutifully followed behind them, but couldn't help feeling preoccupied.

'Come on, Bethany, you do one,' Mr Chase suggested.

'Um, I'm OK. Thanks anyway, Dad.'

She sat down on a step and pulled out her book from her bag.

'It's fun,' her mother said, still sniggering at the picture of Mr Chase looking like he was wearing Nelson's Column as a hat. 'Try one. Make it look like you're pushing the statue over.'

Bethany looked up and smiled. 'It's OK, Mum. You go ahead.'

Mr and Mrs Chase exchanged a brief glance and quietly sighed.

'We're on holiday,' Mr Chase said, sitting down on the steps by his daughter. 'You don't have to read your books or any of that stuff. We're here to enjoy ourselves. That's the whole point of a holiday.'

'I know,' Bethany replied.

'It's just . . . you've been working very hard at school all year. And . . . well, it's really good that you're reading so much. But you do seem to read an awful lot of these books.' He tapped the cover of the book Bethany was holding. '*Encyclopaedia of Supernatural Beings in British Folklore*. Wow. Exciting.'

'*Dad*. I don't make fun of the books you read,' she said defensively.

'OK, I know. I'm sorry. What I mean is —'

Mrs Chase interrupted. 'What your father means is that you've become obsessed with all this spirit and supernatural stuff. And maybe it's not healthy.'

'But I'm trying to . . .' Bethany trailed off. She wanted to explain to her parents that she needed to find some answers to her questions. If she hadn't imagined a spirit realm, and it was all true, then she should know how it worked. She had to make sense of it.

Mrs Chase smiled. 'Maybe it's time to concentrate on having fun in the real world for a change. You know, like you used to. You used to love joking around. You used to love taking these sorts of photos.'

Bethany opened her mouth to protest, but found herself unable to speak. This wasn't the first time she'd had this conversation with her parents. Her cheeks flushed red with embarrassment. *It was true. She had stopped having fun. Ever since last summer she had become serious as if it would help her cope with what had happened.*

'Come on,' Mr Chase said, standing up. 'Let's put this away and get some ice cream. My treat.'

He reached out for the book and Bethany reluctantly passed it over to him. He put it in his backpack and held her hand. Her mum held her other hand as they hurried over to the ice-cream van. 'First one there gets a chocolate flake,' he said, running ahead.

'You're cheating,' Bethany shouted, managing to grab tightly on to his hand and pull him back.

Mrs Chase did the same. 'Typical man, can't stick to the rules. Keep a hold, Bethany,' she said, then sprinted off to the ice-cream van ahead of them, laughing hysterically. 'Thanks,' she called over her shoulder.

'Not fair,' Bethany complained, and started laughing as well.

'I don't know. Some people have no shame,' Mr Chase sighed.

The ice-cream vendor viewed them with weary disdain as they giggled breathlessly. Bethany and her mum kept changing the flavour they wanted, pestering Mr Chase until he finally relented and bought them both chocolate flakes, although he ended up in a long and confusing conversation about squirty syrup with the vendor.

As Bethany tucked into her double chocolate ice cream, thinking that maybe her parents were right and it was best to enjoy herself for a change, a glimmer of movement caught her eye among the legs of the passing tourists.

It can't be, Bethany thought, peering at the animal with complete and utter bewilderment. *Surely there was no way it could have followed her here all by itself?*

Sitting there on the pavement of Trafalgar Square, miles from Aunt Bess's house, was the black cat with the eerie orange eyes. It was staring directly at Bethany.

She made a move towards the cat but her mother pulled her in the opposite direction towards the fountains. 'Come on, we need to get a photo. We'll do one by the lion statues.'

'But . . .' Bethany murmured.

'I know,' Mr Chase said. 'Make it look like you're feeding the statue your ice cream.'

'Yes, that's a good one,' Mrs Chase agreed.

When Bethany turned back round, the cat had vanished and, despite the summer sunshine, she felt a deep chill run through her.

'Hold it,' Mr Chase called out. 'And ssmmiillee.'

Bethany tried her best to fake a grin.

It didn't take long for the cat to appear again. Several times that day, it turned up in completely different locations. It followed them along a path on the bank of the Thames, where it scampered along walls and through railings to keep up with them, before being scared off by a screeching toddler. Hours later it reappeared as they stopped to admire the music of a busker playing a violin. It weaved through the crowd of tourists to stare deliberately at Bethany again.

'Different class of busker here,' Mr Chase joked as Bethany kept her gaze focused on the strange feline.

She was sure that was the last time they'd see it. They had changed trains on the underground twice and they were on the escalator coming out of the station when they heard the queue of people behind them laughing in surprise and talking excitedly to one another. They were all taking it in turn to move out of the way as the black cat purposefully ran up the stairs of the escalator.

'Look,' Mrs Chase said, noticing the disruption. 'How funny, someone's cat must have escaped.'

'Maybe it's been looking for mice,' a stranger remarked wryly.

'That's the black cat from Aunt Bess's house,' Bethany said, but her voice was drowned out by the laughing adults.

Mrs Chase misheard her daughter and replied, 'Yes, we could take it back. I'm sure she wouldn't notice another one.'

Bethany wanted to explain, but was distracted as a young woman in pink glasses picked the cat up and looked for some sort of name tag. The animal squirmed in her arms and stared meaningfully at Bethany.

'You really do see all sorts in London, don't you?' remarked Mr Chase as he walked through the barriers.

Bethany rushed out of the station. There was no way a normal cat could follow her around the city of London, she knew. The question was not *how* it was following her, but *why*?

Bethany led her parents away from the tube station and through an area of old-fashioned lanes with modern shop fronts. Mr and Mrs Chase were keen to stop and browse at some of the more attractive window displays, but Bethany kept dragging them round the next corner. Before long, they became lost in a maze of identical streets and Mrs Chase threw up her hands. 'OK, enough! I'm exhausted. I vote we stop for coffee and cake.'

'Maybe just a few more streets?' Bethany suggested, glancing uncertainly over her shoulder. She tried to herd her fatigued parents up the next road. Ideally, she wanted to find somewhere with lots of doors that could be closed. Her parents had different ideas, though, and drifted to the entrance of a nearby café.

The café was modern and stylish. Customers were gathered around the cramped tables, engrossed in their newspapers and magazines, trying their hardest to ignore each other. Mr Chase was busily admiring a huge glass cake stand that was the centrepiece of the café, each layer laden with plump cakes and glossy pastries.

Bethany, agitated, checked the street for any signs of the four-legged pursuer before she finally took a seat beside her parents.

'Where do you get your energy from?' her mother sighed. 'I know I was saying you need to have more fun, but you can rest in between times, you know.'

Bethany smiled weakly. 'You know, you're right. Maybe I should read my book for a bit.' She rummaged through her father's bag and found the encyclopaedia, quickly flicking through the pages until she found a relevant section on animals. There were references to cats used as familiars by witches and sorcerers, cats that signified bad luck, cats that represented spirit guides. All the comments seemed to be negative and cautionary but there was nothing specific about black cats that followed you around London and stared at you with eerie orange eyes.

Bethany peeked out of the café window. She wondered what the woman in the pink glasses had done with it. Could you hand in cats at underground stations like lost property? Or would she have taken it to some cat refuge? She felt increasingly worried. *It wasn't a normal cat. Normal cats couldn't follow you like that. But what did it want? Why was it after her?*

Just as Bethany felt they might have shaken it free, she caught sight of it. The cat was sitting by a lamppost outside the café, casually licking its paws. It glanced directly at her.

'Right, that's it.' She pushed back her seat and started towards the door, but she stopped in her tracks. As she peered round the café she felt her head reel at the bizarre sight before her. Several customers appeared to have Quinn's head on their shoulders, replacing their own faces. The identical Quinn heads were frozen in a grinning expression and were facing Bethany. It took her a moment to realise what she was looking at: the customers were all reading the same magazine and were holding it in front of them in such a way that it covered their faces. The cover was a full-size picture of Quinn's head with his impossibly wide grin, mischievous eyes and quiff of pink hair.

The Quinn faces winked at her.

She smiled, feeling briefly reassured by his face. 'Quinn?' she said, as if hoping that he could answer back.

The strange illusion was broken as the various customers shifted position. The gentleman nearest Bethany placed the magazine on to the table and picked up his shopping to

21

leave. At that moment Bethany noticed the black cat moving to the entrance of the café and sneezing three times very precisely in her direction. A single orange fell free from the shopping bag of the man leaving the café and rolled towards the till, lodging under the foot of a passing waiter carrying a tray of dirty cups. His legs wobbled comically as he slipped on it and he was sent flying backwards into the giant cake stand at the centre of the café. He hit it with such force that the entire structure swayed left, then right, then the whole thing toppled down to the ground. Jammy sponges, chocolate éclairs, cream cakes, gateaux, roulades and meringues were catapulted across the café. The glass stand landed with an almighty crashing sound.

No one moved for several seconds and Bethany looked in disbelief at the scene of chaos. The falling stand had narrowly missed both her parents, but it had crushed the chair that she had been sitting in moments before. Turning, she saw the cat slinking away from the café, a distinctly satisfied expression on its face.

As the dust settled, Mr and Mrs Chase looked over at her. They were covered in an assortment of cakes. An entire chocolate gateau had landed on Mr Chase's head and sloped sideways like a large, elaborate hat. Mrs Chase picked at a cherry bakewell that drooped over her eye. 'An interesting way to serve cakes,' she noted drolly.

Bethany didn't speak on the tube back to Aunt Bess's house. Her thoughts were in a whirl. She didn't really understand how or why she had narrowly avoided death by cakes but she was sure the signs were ominous. The spirit realm seemed to be intervening in the real world and that couldn't be good. The cat, whatever it was, was capable of magic, and not the nice sort.

Her parents were unaware of their daughter's agitation and were too busy laughing at each other dressed in staff shirts given to them by the café. They were returning during rush hour and the carriages were filled with people. Bethany barely noticed the journey back, worrying about what she was going to do. She was pulled from her thoughts abruptly as Mr Chase said, 'Quinn?'

Bethany's head jerked up. 'What? What did you just say?'

Mr Chase had picked up a magazine a previous passenger had left behind on their seat and was examining it intently. 'Odd-looking chap, isn't he?' he remarked, showing Bethany the front cover. It was a picture of Quinn.

'You can see him too?' Bethany asked. She had assumed that Quinn had used magic to appear on the magazines, magic that only she could see. *I mean, it would be madness for him to actually display himself on a magazine cover for everyone to look at. Why would he do that?* Even for him, that would be strange.

'Of course I can,' her father laughed. 'Is he from a film or something? He looks quite a character.'

'Um . . . yeah. Yeah, I think so,' Bethany lied. 'Can I have a look at that a moment?'

As her father passed it over she could see that it was the same magazine she had noticed the customers reading in the café. And, she realised, it was probably what she had seen her first day in London – someone holding the magazine up in the street as they waited to cross the road. She looked at the picture of him now and found it strange to see him up close. It looked like the head of a fat man but weirdly smooth and artificial as if it wasn't a proper photograph. His grin was exceptionally wide and curled into a brilliant smile. The caption on the cover read: *Here Comes Quinn*. Eagerly, Bethany flicked through it for some more information, but she was interrupted as her mother clutched her hand.

'This is our stop,' Mrs Chase said, yanking Bethany to the doors. The magazine fell from her grip.

'But I need to read that!' Bethany insisted.

Her parents were already stepping off the train, though, and they pulled Bethany on to the platform with them. When she looked at the departing train, she could see several people holding up the same magazine. An old granny, a large biker with tattooed arms and a young man with lots of gold jewellery – all were transformed momentarily into grinning Quinns.

CHAPTER THREE

THE MINERAL UNDERGROUND

'Well, I must say that's . . . that's terrible,' Aunt Bess said, as soon as Bethany's parents had finished explaining the incident in the café. She coughed several times and quietly apologised.

Bethany used the opportunity to sneak off to her bedroom, artfully stepping between the clumped mass of dogs and cats. She could hear her dad already exaggerating the story for dramatic effect, although he had conveniently overlooked the fact that the cake stand had come crashing down on the chair Bethany had just been sitting in. Bethany had to fight the urge to tell her parents and aunt about the real culprit. They wouldn't believe her about the cat, she knew, or that magic was involved. It didn't matter. What mattered now was that she protect herself.

If it's attacked me once, it'll probably attack again, Bethany reasoned. She needed to be ready if it did. But why was it after her? Maybe it wasn't attacking her at all, maybe it was just a coincidence that the cake stand had fallen over. *No. There was definitely something shifty about the way it behaved, almost too clever for a cat.*

She quickly closed the door to her cramped bedroom and retrieved a drawstring bag from her suitcase. Untying the string she upended the contents on to her bed. A collection of lucky charms, pendants and talismans fell out, along with some sprigs of rosemary, several crystals and a small bottle of holy water. *Better safe than sorry*, she thought.

Ever since her strange adventure in the spirit hotel Bethany had scoured books on the supernatural about ways to protect herself against malicious spirits. Her memories of the demon had left her terrified and uneasy and she wanted to make sure she had some way to repel an attack if it ever came to that. The advice she had found was often contradictory and confusing, but it had led to her collecting all types of charms and protective pendants just in case. She felt it best that she was prepared for any eventuality, however unlikely.

Her mind drifted to the memory of that moment she had seen the demon escaping, the black flame emerging from the mirror, slipping away before it could be caught. The thought made her shiver.

Bethany flung a selection of talismans around her neck and placed the sprigs of rosemary over the door and window.

She shoved the crystals in her pocket and, uncertain how she should use the holy water, emptied the contents on to her hands then flicked the rest liberally round the room. It was as she was doing this that she saw two orbs of orange glowing outside her window. Bethany jumped on to the bed and looked through the pane. Directly across from her, perched on the neighbour's windowsill, was the black cat, calmly examining Bethany.

'I'm on to you!' she shouted across. 'I've got protection now.' She waved a handful of the pendants at the cat menacingly, laughing in a way that was supposed to sound confident but actually sounded a little demented. 'That's right! No more tricks.'

The cat seemed largely unimpressed by this performance, and it took Bethany a full minute to realise that a short, elderly woman in a flowery dress was looking out from the window opposite with an expression of confusion and shock.

'Oh no, I didn't mean you,' Bethany tried to explain, mouthing the words. 'It's the cat.' She tried pointing at the cat, but her neighbour promptly pulled the curtains shut. Bethany scowled at the animal, cursing it before pulling the curtains across her window.

She sighed heavily and slumped down on the bed, feeling anxious and frustrated. Idly, she pawed at the remaining charms and talismans on the bed. Among the pile of lucky symbols she noticed a neat white card with green writing on it. She didn't remember having seen it before and wondered where she had picked it up from.

It read: *PLEASE TURN OVER FOR HELP*.

She flipped the card over and read the message on the other side: *HELP IS ON THE WAY.*

Bethany couldn't help but groan at the card. 'Ha ha,' she muttered sarcastically. It must have been a joke card she had picked up from somewhere by accident, although she didn't find it very funny. She put it back down in the clutter of objects and was about to get up from the bed when she frowned in surprise.

Bethany held the card up for closer inspection to check she wasn't seeing things. It now read: *NO, HELP REALLY IS ON THE WAY.*

She turned the card over once more: *ALL IN GOOD TIME. PLEASE BE PATIENT.*

Bethany let out a strangled yelping sound. Her stomach lurched with the horrible realisation that she was witnessing actual magic. The card fell from her numb fingers, spinning round as it dropped to the floor, a single word appearing on each side as it fluttered down.

HELP
IS
ON
THE
WAY
PLEASE
STOP
PANICKING!

She ran from the room and screeched as she tripped over

the animals gathered outside her door. There were howls and miaows and barks as Bethany tumbled into the pack and banged her head on the floor. She heard several sets of footsteps running up the stairs and her aunt's voice becoming stern above her. 'Bernard, down. Caspar, away. Meeps, away. All of you – tssst, shoo!'

The animals dispersed and Aunt Bess helped Bethany sit up. 'I'm sorry about that, Bethany. They have a dreadful habit of sitting still when they need to move, and vice versa.'

Mr and Mrs Chase peered over her shoulder. 'Bethany, are you OK?' her mother asked.

'The card . . . the cat . . . I mean, I think something's gone wrong, it must be why Quinn is . . .' Bethany stopped babbling and registered the adult faces staring at her with incomprehension and concern. 'I'm fine,' she corrected herself. 'I just came rushing out.'

'You didn't bang your head too hard, did you?' her father asked.

Bethany stood up and did her best to look completely normal. 'No. I'm fine.'

'Well, if you're sure,' Mrs Chase said, cautiously.

Bethany joined her parents and Aunt Bess downstairs. They all shared a dinner of lasagne and garlic bread, Mr and Mrs Chase examining each mouthful of food for possible cat hairs, while Bethany tried not to let her thoughts dwell on that day's events.

When it was time to go to bed, she reluctantly returned to her room. The card, she noticed with some relief, was lying untouched on the floor where it had fallen and was now completely blank. She checked the window several times to see if the cat was there but it seemed to have vanished, although twice she thought she saw two orange eyes glinting among the garden plants. Finally, Bethany settled, and tried to let her mind slip off into sleep.

Her thoughts were disrupted with fleeting visions of a demon and spirits being drained of their power. She woke several times, cold sweat clinging to her back, her heart hammering in her chest. When she did at last make it to the verge of deep sleep, her dreaming mind conjured up the sound of a train approaching. It came to a stop nearby, a bell making a precise *ding-ding* noise before opening its doors and letting several passengers shuffle out.

'So . . . is this where we are then?' a voice said – a distinctly Irish-sounding voice.

'Yes,' another voice replied patiently, sighing.

'She looks a little different,' a third added.

'Are you sure it's her now?' the fourth voice asked.

'How many people did you give that card to?' replied the second.

'Ah, you've got a point there, so you do.'

The first voice piped up again. 'Do you think she knows anything yet? You know, about Quinn and —'

'Shut up, Donovan!' the second voice shouted.

'Sorry, Flannigan. I just meant —'

Bethany awoke in an instant, realising that this was no dream she was having and that she knew these voices.

30

Flannigan, Seamus, Pat and Donovan. The shock of hearing them hit her like a flash. 'Leprechauns!' Bethany uttered aloud. She sat bolt upright.

For the briefest moment she caught sight of four human shapes, no bigger than her hand and with disproportionately large heads, standing on the flat edge of the largest box near her bed. The figures consisted of a faint green light and their definition flickered tenuously like candle flames caught in a strong wind. She could see faces fizzing with brighter sparks of light, stretching and blurring, as if they were having trouble maintaining their form. They looked as though they were in pain.

'I told you this was dangerous. She's stopped believing in us.'

Bethany felt her thoughts fighting, part of her unable to believe what she was seeing, part of her recollecting the band of devious yet loyal spirits. 'Flannigan,' she said, addressing the largest green blur. 'It *is* you, isn't it?'

Almost immediately, the leprechaun gained definition. 'How many other leprechauns do you know?' he replied sharply, then laughed. 'Of course it's me.'

'Seamus? Pat? Donovan?' Each of the three leprechauns shimmered and surged with light, the patches of green resolving into grinning faces. All sighed with relief. Donovan still looked young compared to the others, freckle-faced and with only a small tuft for a beard. Pat seemed mostly hair in comparison, flowing from underneath his low hat, whereas Seamus was somewhere between the two, with a beaming expressive face that ended in a long beard.

'What are you doing here?' Bethany asked, unable to hide her amazement. It was strange seeing them like this, small and ghostly and not entirely real.

'You called us,' replied Flannigan.

'Called you? I didn't call . . . oh, the card,' Bethany said. 'That was *you*?'

'It was Pat's idea. See, we keep an eye on you from time to time. Thought you might need a way of contacting us if the moment arrived.' Flannigan shrugged his shoulders and smiled. 'Which is a happy coincidence when you think about it.'

'What do you mean?' Bethany asked, puzzled.

Seamus and Pat were moving a large pot on to its side formed from the same strange spirit light as them. It was a bulbous round thing and resembled a cauldron in shape, except that its contents glowed with a lustrous golden colour.

'No time to explain,' Flannigan said. 'You need to come with us.'

'Come with you where?' Bethany said. 'Is this something to do with the black cat and Quinn?'

The leprechauns peered up simultaneously.

'You've seen Quinn?' Donovan asked nervously. 'She's seen Quinn,' he repeated to the others.

'Shut up, Donovan,' Flannigan snapped.

'It was just pictures of him, but I think he's trying to get in touch in some way,' Bethany explained.

Flannigan was gesturing to the others. 'We need to go now. Transmigrate her.'

Bethany remembered that word and knew what it meant. She jumped out of her bed and backed away from the leprechauns, wagging her finger at them. 'Oh no, you don't. I'm not going anywhere,' she told them firmly. 'I'm staying in my body.'

'It's a completely standard procedure,' Flannigan reassured her.

'Fairly harmless,' insisted Seamus.

'It's only ever gone wrong twice,' Pat added. He had moved the pot on to its side and a beam of golden light leaped out at Bethany, making her feel as if she was caught in the glare of a searchlight. Donovan laughed madly, ran to the pot and dived in. There was an erupting flash and the young leprechaun was sent hurtling towards Bethany.

'Well, it's been really nice catching up. Feel free to drop by anytime soon,' she said, as she turned to flee the room. Something heavy knocked into her, though, and she felt winded with the force of the blow. Bethany fell backwards on to the bed, her legs, arms and head tingling strangely. She found she was staring at someone, someone that looked exactly like her, wearing her pyjamas and scrutinising her with interest. 'It worked!' the imposter said, gazing at her.

'What is going on?' Bethany demanded. She knew, though, as soon as she looked at herself and saw that she was made up of a bright gauzy light that she had been removed from her body and was in her spirit form. The sensation was every bit as disorientating as she remembered it. She held out her hands and could see through their pink glow to the floor below her. She peered up at her physical body and could distinguish the faint outline of Donovan's spirit superimposed over it. 'No. No, you're not doing this. Put me back now! Donovan, get out of there this minute!'

She felt an unpleasant mixture of anger and panic: anger that she wasn't being listened to, panic that she was stepping over into a world of strange and terrifying possibilities. *I don't want this. I don't want to go to the spirit realm.* 'Put me back!' she screeched in a fury, getting up from the bed.

'Just following orders,' Flannigan told her. He nodded at Pat, who took a handful of powder from the pouch on his belt and threw it over Bethany's spirit body. *'Yeartha don toory.'*

'Don't you dare,' Bethany growled at him, too late, and felt an unpleasant shrinking sensation as if she were having her spirit body crushed down into a denser form. She looked in horror at Pat, Seamus and Flannigan as she shrivelled down to their size. Flannigan ran over to her and grabbed her by the arm. He looked brighter now, more defined, and she could see that he was eager to leave. 'We need to go,' he informed her.

Bethany felt overwhelmed. Her head swayed. There was a curious effect of stepping into the spirit realm that meant the physical world seemed less substantial and real. 'What's all this about? Whose orders are you following?' Then she remembered how cross she was. 'I don't care, I don't need to know. I'm not going anywhere,' she said assertively.

'Of course not,' Flannigan said, pulling her towards the window. 'I respect that.'

Pat and Seamus were each grabbing the handle of the pot and dragging it after them urgently. Bethany could see that there was a shape waiting by the windowsill, much more obvious now she was in her spirit body. She was too busy examining the sight to notice that she was being hurried forwards. At first glance, she could make out a line of tiny windows hanging in mid-air, with peculiar figures looking out of them. On closer inspection, she realised these windows belonged to the carriages of a train, although the train must have been hidden by magic as it was so perfectly camouflaged that only its outline was visible against the night sky. It was on the same scale as the leprechauns and had parked against the bedroom windowsill as if stopping at a platform.

Ding-ding the bell sounded. Several carriage doors opened and Flannigan bundled Bethany through the nearest doorway before she could protest, then quickly helped Pat and Seamus haul the pot on board. The interior of the carriage was sleek and elegant, formed from some dark, partially transparent substance that was studded with glittering, precious jewels. Double seats were lined up against the wall and several passengers were sitting at the far end, craning their necks to get a look at Bethany. She failed to notice the attention she was receiving as she gazed out at the giant version of herself in the bedroom. 'I'll look after your body,' Donovan called out to her cheerfully in her own voice.

'You might find some of this a bit strange,' Flannigan warned her as the train pulled off.

'Oh, really?' she replied sarcastically. 'What could possibly be strange about any of *this*?'

'Keep your hand on one of the diamonds,' he told her. The leprechauns had each grabbed one of the jewelled clusters that were sticking out of the carriage walls, holding them as casually as if they were holding a handrail.

'I'm not doing anything you say until you explain what is going on,' Bethany replied stubbornly, folding her arms. Her panic was deepening and she needed to make a stand before events were completely out of her control. *They can't do this*, she told herself.

Unfortunately, the train gained speed at that moment, swiftly shooting upwards at such a sharp angle that Bethany was thrown down the aisle. The train swerved to the right, then dipped, then jerked to the left. The speed with which the turns were made would have been impossible for a normal train — even if it could move without tracks — but Bethany remembered this was a product of the spirit realm and nothing behaved in a remotely normal manner. It felt like being on board a rollercoaster that had veered out of control and was moments away from crashing in a spectacular fashion. As it hurtled downwards and she fell all the way back along the carriage, Flannigan caught her and guided her hand on to a cluster of diamonds. She found it had the unusual effect of completely anchoring her to the spot, despite the sudden changes in direction.

'This is the Mineral Underground,' he explained gleefully, clearly enjoying the chaotic zigzag journey. 'It's going to take us back to our city. Just after we pick up some gold in your world.'

'Right,' Bethany said, dazed and not completely aware of what he was telling her. 'Of course.'

The train carried out a series of sickening turns and the leprechauns roared with laughter, which caused patches of four-leafed clover to sprout across the nearby seats. In seconds, they were high above London and the world below them had drastically changed appearance. Instead of just a grid of streets and a patchwork of buildings, the city glowed with a dizzying array of spirit forms. There were thick patches of darkness and light moving in fluid patterns like the swirls and eddies of a river. Caught up in these thick currents were thousands upon thousands of flickering lights, tiny and precious and each shining with its own unique display. By the sheer amount of these lights and the way they moved, Bethany guessed that these were the people of the city And there were all sorts of spirits moving among them. There were fox spirits and rat spirits. There were majestic, angelic entities, and dark ghoulish beings, and the faded blue imprints of ghosts. There were spirits that had sly appearances, bright spirits that shone with vibrant colours, and ones that swooped over the streets like diving birds. The city was every bit as fascinating and impressive in the spirit realm as it was in the physical realm.

She glimpsed all of this briefly as the train fell in a corkscrew manoeuvre and then swerved at a ninety-degree angle. Her spirit body reacted to these sudden drops and turns by taking on an unhealthy green tone. 'Is there any particular reason we can't travel in a normal way?' she gulped after it became clear the train was following a random path.

Flannigan tried not to laugh at her sickly pallor. 'Cities are always difficult to negotiate. We can't risk being seen by people so the train moves along an invisible route. Even at night that's tricky.' He noticed Bethany's blank expression and elaborated, 'It's dangerous for us to be seen in this form. Most of your kind don't believe in us and whenever we're seen by someone who doesn't believe in us, well . . . we stop existing for a short time. It's very painful. I certainly wouldn't recommend it.'

The train plummeted down until it reached ground level, snaking through the walls of buildings and ducking beneath floorboards. As it passed through objects in the physical world it gave Bethany the unpleasant feeling of being plunged through cold water, and she groaned as it moved through several walls in quick succession. Pat and Seamus seemed oblivious to this and had let go of the diamond handrails so that they could move their sizeable pot towards the nearest door. Flannigan pulled down the window and peeked out. Up ahead, among the swirls and streaks of spirit energy surrounding the physical world, there was a pulsing point of golden light. 'OK, not far,' he shouted out to his friends.

Seamus and Pat wedged the door open and lowered the pot outside the carriage so that it was dragged along by the side of the speeding train. They managed to keep hold of it as the train shot up the edge of a drainpipe, rushed across a slate roof and dived through several bedrooms. For some reason, they were both finding this dangerous procedure hilarious and laughed maniacally as they leaned out of the door at a perilous angle.

'You're going to have to be quick with this one,' Flannigan shouted at them. 'It's nearly manifested.'

Bethany watched as the point of golden light came into view. It was floating above a sleeping figure, a balding gentleman whose skinny feet dangled out of the end of his bed. The sphere of lustrous gold was sending out brief pulses of energy that seemed to be connecting with the man's spirit, illuminating it in bright flashes, far brighter than any other object in the spirit realm.

'Nearly,' Flannigan said urgently.

Pat had resorted to holding Seamus by the ankles so that Seamus could swing the pot in a scooping motion like a large net. The train lunged forward in one last burst of energy.

'NOW!' screeched Flannigan.

Seamus pulled the pot in a wide arc as the carriage passed over the sleeping man. It swung upwards, perfectly timed, and netted the point of golden light. The entire train cheered and Flannigan punched the air. 'Perfect,' he bellowed proudly.

If the sleeping man had woken at that precise moment he would have caught the briefest glimpse of a miniature train, barely discernable from its surroundings, carrying a selection of small mischievous passengers who were struggling with a pot of glowing gold. This struck Bethany as so absurd that she burst into a fit of giggles and couldn't contain herself for several moments. Pat pulled Seamus back into the carriage, reeling him in like a prize catch. The train dropped down under the ground, finally easing off from its frantic pace.

Flannigan watched Bethany laughing. 'Well, thank goodness. For a moment there, I was thinking you would never cheer up.'

CHAPTER FOUR

THE STOLEN CITY

The four of them sat around the pot and admired its contents. The golden light inside swirled and surged enticingly, forming vague and tantalising patterns. Bethany's last experience of gold in the spirit realm had been the golden strands of the Spellbound Hotel that had proved deadly to anyone who touched them. This was different, though. There was nothing sinister about this gold. It gave off a brilliant light, a light that seemed to warm Bethany's spirit just by looking at it.

'What is it?' she said, genuinely awestruck. There seemed to be something alive about the glowing contents of the pot.

Flannigan managed to drag his gaze away. The train was moving at a steady pace below ground, stopping to drop off and pick up more of the strange passengers, and everyone was glancing greedily at the pot. 'This is gold,' he said in a quiet voice. 'Not like the gold of your world. It is something much more precious: this is pure magic.'

As if to confirm this, the surface of the gilded light vibrated, creating a display of dancing shapes: bands, beads, stars, spheres. The forms shifted and scampered playfully.

'This is the very essence of all the magic in the spirit realm *and* the physical realm,' Flannigan continued. 'It shapes realities. It is, without doubt, the most powerful substance in all the universes.'

Bethany looked at him. 'You said *universes*.'

He nodded his head. 'Oh yes. There is more than one universe. And more than one world. Which is why this comes in so useful.' He tapped the pot.

Bethany peered back into the shifting gold. 'So what does it do exactly? This gold?'

'Do?' Flannigan echoed. He smiled at her the way that very old, wise people smile at the young. Bethany found it infuriating. 'This,' Flannigan said patiently, 'can change the future. When we caught this it was passing through into the physical realm. It manifests as the magic of your world. More often than not it becomes a completely unique idea. Sometimes it is pure luck.'

'But it was attaching to that man,' she said, thinking of the way it was sending out flashes of gold.

'Yes. And that man's life would have been changed for ever. It might have been something wonderful he invented

42

that would have altered the world in some powerful way, or some subtler form of luck that would have irrevocably changed the course of his life, that in turn would affect hundreds of other lives that would alter the course of the future. Magic has a strange life of its own.'

'But you stole it!' Bethany said accusingly.

Flannigan became defensive. 'Of course we stole it. If any spirit is going to steal it it's going to be a leprechaun. It's our job.'

Pat and Seamus both nodded their heads thoughtfully. 'You're right there. It is our job,' they agreed.

'But you shouldn't be stealing it,' Bethany scolded them. 'Why do you need the gold anyway?'

'Well, we've got to have gold,' Flannigan said, folding his arms. 'It's how we maintain the balance. It's how we keep order. I mean, someone's got to regulate it, you know.'

He looked suitably upset by her comments, as if no one had ever questioned his thinking on this subject. There was not much point in arguing with him, Bethany realised, especially about something she didn't fully understand. Instead, she turned her attention to more pressing matters. 'You still haven't said if this is anything to do with the cat or Quinn. That's all I'm worried about at the moment.'

At the mention of Quinn, the entire carriage fell silent and the other passengers began to peer over curiously. Flannigan's face tightened. 'Ah,' he whispered nervously. 'It's probably best you don't mention his name at the moment.'

'What – Quinn? Has something happened to him?' Bethany asked, concerned.

'He's fine,' Flannigan reassured her. 'I'll explain later.'

Bethany noticed how uncomfortable Flannigan looked with the reactions they were receiving. Passengers were turning their heads and nudging each other. She could hear her name being mentioned in surprised gasps. It took a few moments to sink in. 'Do they . . . do they know me? I think they just said my name.'

Flannigan's discomfort vanished and he uttered a loud belly laugh. 'Every leprechaun knows *you*, Bethany. You destroyed an extremely powerful demon, a demon that no other spirit could touch. You, *a human*.' He laughed again. 'You're a legend in our world.'

'But . . .' She felt foolish. Her face blushed a deep maroon and the colour seeped down her spirit body. 'Really? I mean, no . . . you can't be serious. That stuff . . . I didn't really do anything.'

'Now, now, we'll have none of that,' Seamus added. 'You should be proud. Destroying that demon was no small feat. You're gifted.' The leprechauns nodded unanimously.

But I didn't destroy the demon, Bethany wanted to shout out, remembering the black shape she had seen escaping. 'You know, I didn't really —'

Before she could finish, the train jerked to a halt and a single figure strode through the doors nearest them. He wore a neat black suit, a simple black hat and carried a formal black pot as if carrying a briefcase, lending him a

44

sombre, official appearance. He took a seat opposite Bethany, and there was something about his presence that made Pat, Seamus and Flannigan sit to attention.

'Ah, Hurm Igrig. How are you, sir?' Flannigan said, adjusting his hat and nodding his head meekly. There was a strained aspect to his voice.

Bethany looked at the figure. He had a similar build to the other leprechauns, but with a wide misshapen head that resembled a particularly knobbly potato in the process of sprouting, one that had somehow formed into a glum, jowly face. His nose was a massive bulbous lump with several warts growing off it and his bushy grey eyebrows were collected in such a deep frown that it was impossible to see his eyes, never mind which direction they were looking in.

'Hmm? Is that . . . hmff . . . now then . . .' He had a gruff tone. 'Is that . . . Finnigan, eh?'

'Flannigan, sir,' the leprechaun corrected.

Hurm Igrig tutted. 'Flannigan,' he repeated. He removed his hat and scratched his brow as if lost in deep thought. 'Flannigan. Gold retrieval. Department of Precious Magic. This is correct?'

'The very same, sir,' Flannigan beamed.

Hurm Igrig grumbled to himself, acknowledging the pot full of gold with a cursory glance. Bethany tried not to stare. He was particularly striking, not only because of his large nose and misshapen face, but also due to an immaculately coiffured head of black and silvery hair that he revealed as he rested his hat on his lap. He brushed a hand through it absentmindedly. 'And you, young lady?' he said, addressing Bethany. 'I do not recollect seeing you before on the Mineral Underground. Forgive me, but you appear to be *human*.'

There seemed to be a vague tone of accusation in his voice. Bethany's spirit body was indeed different to the leprechauns', nimbler and without the exaggerated proportions, yet also casting a colourful light brighter than the other passengers. Self-consciously, she pulled herself back into her seat. 'My name's Bethany Chase,' she said cautiously. She looked at Flannigan for support, but the older leprechaun was doing a bad job at hiding his nervousness.

Hurm Igrig leaned forward. From the dark fold of his brow she could sense that his eyes were scrutinising her. His frown deepened. The rest of the train became tense and quiet. Eventually he pulled a small pad from his pocket and scribbled several notes, tutting and grumbling to himself, then slipped the pad back into his pocket.

That can't be good, Bethany thought.

'Demon slayer,' Hurm Igrig stated abruptly.

'Erm . . . sorry?' Bethany replied, feeling flustered.

'Bethany Chase,' Hurm Igrig said more seriously, as if he was explaining something very simple to her. '*The slayer of demons*. I assume that is you, yes?'

'Um . . . well . . .'

'I'm surprised you do not have your flaming sword with you,' he remarked.

'My what? I . . .' Bethany looked to Flannigan for help.

The leprechaun gave a shrill, forced laugh and jumped to her defence.

'Can you believe it, sir? Isn't she something?' Flannigan said excitedly. 'All of us leprechauns owe her a debt.'

Hurm Igrig faced them without the slightest reaction.

'Well, we'll not bother you any more, Hurm Igrig,' Flannigan said as the train stopped to pick up several more passengers. Mercifully, one of the spirits waved at Hurm Igrig, who reluctantly moved down the carriage to join them. The leprechauns all relaxed with a palpable sense of relief as soon as he was out of range. Pat and Seamus shared a knowing glance.

'What did he mean "slayer of demons"?' Bethany asked in an angry whisper. 'And what was that about a flaming sword?'

'Nothing to worry about,' Flannigan said in a hushed tone. 'To be honest, we may have exaggerated a little about what happened in the hotel. Just a few details here and there. You know, to make you sound better. Nothing serious.'

Seamus gave her the thumbs up. 'For dramatic effect,' he added reassuringly.

Pat jerked his head in the direction of Hurm Igrig. 'Bit of a coincidence, is it not, Flannigan?' he commented.

The older leprechaun nervously fidgeted with a chunky ring on his right hand. He begrudgingly agreed. 'You're not wrong there.'

Bethany could feel her temper rising. 'But why did you have to lie about me?'

Seamus waved her question away as if it was an irrelevance. 'That's Hurm Igrig. A very important leprechaun. And not someone to get on the wrong side of, if you know what I mean.'

Bethany didn't really know what Seamus meant at all, but the train went into a nosedive at that moment and she had to grab hold of the diamonds to prevent herself from falling. The carriage plummeted vertically downwards, accelerating into the earth. They passed through subterranean layers of London, through the foundations of buildings, through underground networks of tunnels, through pipes, then down through the layers of bedrock, passing deeper into the ground until they were moving through layers of different coloured rock. The whole train juddered and shook, the spirit passengers all holding on to the diamonds with the slightly bored expression of commuters returning home after a hard day at work.

Bethany watched with fascination as the rock outside the carriage window became darker and gradually denser until they were moving through pitch blackness. Vague glints of light began to shine ahead of them, brightening and multiplying in the dark until they revealed thick patches of crystals. The crystals glowed mysteriously and appeared in larger clumps, eventually forming the walls of the tunnel. Without warning there was a brilliant surge of light and the train was pulling in to a busy underground station that shone a bright, dazzling white.

'You're about to see something no human has ever seen,'

Seamus told her. 'Well, no human has ever seen and survived.'

'Oh.' Bethany felt the panic return, a tight sensation in her spirit body as if she was being squeezed by an invisible force. She peered out of the window, filled with a dreadful curiosity. A surprisingly normal-looking train station came into view, though, busy with arriving and departing trains, and numerous platforms teeming with the strange little spirits. The train glided through the station and came to a screeching halt at a short platform away from the main hub of activity. The doors opened and the passengers rushed out. There were several sets of stairs leading up towards doorways set at different heights, and everyone was marching up and through them.

'What is this place?' Bethany asked. 'Is it real?'

The three leprechauns were struggling with the pot, dragging it out of the doors and heaving it across the platform. Bethany quickly joined in as they carried it up a steep set of stairs. They seemed to be in a hurry.

'Of course it's real. It's our home,' Flannigan said, straining. He helped Seamus and Pat through the doorway as they made it to the top of the steps. The leprechauns stepped over a threshold with the pot and dropped out of view. 'You next,' he said, ushering her forward. 'We don't want to be late.'

'Late for what?' Bethany asked, but as she went to step through the doorway she hit a barrier that knocked her backwards down a few steps and caused her spirit body to

49

tingle unpleasantly, as if she'd received a mild electric shock.

'Oops. Sorry, my fault,' Flannigan said, helping her up. He produced a ring from his pocket and placed it on Bethany's index finger. The band of gold was decorated with a large green gemstone and she held her hand up admiringly. Flannigan shoved her through the entrance and she saw the gemstone briefly flashing with light as she passed though the invisible barrier. 'Everybody needs a ring now. New security measures after the . . . *incident*,' he explained.

Bethany stumbled forwards. The floor seemed to have disappeared and in its place was a plumply cushioned chair. She landed comfortably and looked over at Pat and Seamus. They were each sitting in a chair that was balanced on the tall, moving legs of a giraffe. Bethany leaned over the edge of her chair and saw that she too was sitting on something that was half chair, half giraffe. It swayed to and fro as it shifted its weight from one leg to another.

'Um . . . so . . . this is high up and weird,' she said in a nervous voice.

Flannigan stepped through the doorway and fell on to a chair too.

'You'll find it best to just hold on tight,' Seamus suggested.

The four chairs immediately began striding forwards in long sloping footsteps. The motion caused Bethany to slide back and forth. Terrified, she clutched the armrests and pushed herself as far into the plush cushioning as she could get.

'You wanted to know what we need the gold for,' Flannigan shouted over.

The chairs trundled to a rocky verge that looked out on to a gigantic cavern. An entire bustling city filled the vast space. Bethany could barely conceive of what she was seeing. It was so fantastic that she nearly slipped from her seat at the mere sight of it. Gigantic stalagmites sprouted upwards from the ground of the cavern, except these formations were buildings of astonishing scale and variety. They were gathered in clusters, hundreds of them in total. There were tall towers that leaned at perilous angles; majestic glass constructions that glittered with chandelier brilliance; immense edifices that were so large they had smaller buildings stuck to their outsides like barnacles on a ship. One ghostly building was formed entirely from a thick mist-like substance, as if a cloud had condensed into an austere design of spires and columns. Beside this was a building so thin that it was nothing more than a spiral stairwell with a single room swaying at its narrow tip.

At the centre of this dizzying display sat a huge gothic construction. It was a complicated structure that looked more like clockwork than an actual building, with numerous floors, turrets and stairwells all moving with steady precision on an assortment of huge interlocking cogs and wheels. It was darker than the other buildings that surrounded it and made Bethany think of an ornate cathedral with its gloomy, dominating presence.

She couldn't linger on the sight for long, though. Her

attention quickly shifted to the traffic of this startling city; the colourful leprechauns in their walking chairs. There were regal pink chairs with flamingo legs, a frumpy armchair with hen feet, seats that scampered along on dog legs, even a dumpy elephant chair that carried several rows of passengers on its back. They all moved along the roads that connected the buildings, but unlike the roads of a normal city these curled and looped in almost every direction, squiggling downwards, bending sideways and coiling upwards, forming a tangled labyrinth of routes between the buildings. Bethany found herself gazing at the scene in amazement, so overwhelmed that she could not speak for several moments.

When she did manage to form coherent sounds again, all she could manage was, 'Woah!' Then again, 'Wooaaahh!'

'This is our home, the Stolen City,' Flannigan explained with a note of pride. 'This is what we do with the gold. Everything you see, even these chairs, is made from that magic.'

'This is . . . this is *incredible*,' Bethany gasped.

Flannigan smiled. 'We've got something really good to show you.'

The giraffe chairs positioned themselves in a line at the edge of a long curving road that led down to the heart of the city. At some unseen signal, they bounded forward. Bethany screeched. The leprechauns whooped with joy.

The chairs galloped down the steep incline and joined the stream of traffic. Bethany found herself among crowded lanes of people. A bewildering parade of characters passed her by. Most of the leprechauns resembled Flannigan, Pat and Seamus, but some of the spirits had extremely ugly features caught in devious expressions, others had delicate pixie-like faces, others looked honest and friendly. Many of them stared at her, nudging each other, pointing, and even waving excitedly at her and calling her name. She noticed several ghosts working for the little people, guiding the larger chairs as if they were chauffeurs, also shrunken in size as Bethany was. They, too, waved.

Bethany did her best to wave back, but her chair was busily joggling her from side to side. She felt an odd mixture of emotions – quite excited at being recognised, as if she was very important, yet also a little nervous at crowds of strange beings calling out to her.

Pat cackled hysterically. He grabbed the pot of gold balancing precariously on his seat as he vaulted over a series of bumps in the road. They raced past a slow moving line of wizened sprites on the backs of turtles, then bounded into several lanes of busy traffic. Seamus jostled for position and caused a panic among the running chairs. The herd thundered forwards and Bethany screamed.

'Good chair. Nice chair,' she said reassuringly, patting an armrest and hoping it would calm her charging seat.

Several people tumbled to the ground in the chaos. Chairs barged into one another. The whole scene was like some bizarre race. Seamus's chair galloped in front of Bethany and guided it down a curling side road, with Pat and Flannigan following behind. In moments they had made it to a collection of tall buildings at the centre of the city. As the chairs halted at a set of stairs, she quickly clambered off and scowled at Flannigan.

'That was not big or clever. I nearly fell off!' she said angrily. 'Is there any way that you travel that is not horrible?'

This seemed to amuse the leprechauns. They descended the steps and hurried along the narrow street. It was full of leprechauns of different types. Bethany could see groups of them making colourful displays of magic as casually as if they were making conversation, while some rushed between buildings, dragging their pots of gold behind them. 'It's just ideas. We like the idea of travelling in walking chairs, so that's why we do it,' Flannigan said. 'You should let yourself enjoy it. It's more fun that way.'

The leprechauns turned a corner. 'Ah-hah. Here we are,' Flannigan exclaimed triumphantly. 'Look,' he said to her, pointing ahead at a statue standing on the plinth in front of them. 'Isn't that something!'

It took Bethany a moment to realise what she was looking at. The statue appeared to be formed entirely from one huge, sculpted diamond. The two figures portrayed were standing in dramatic, heroic poses. Bethany and Quinn had been sculpted as fearless warriors, with Bethany's figure bearing a glowing crown and wielding a sword covered in flames. The Jackomuss demon lay shrivelled at their feet.

She burst into laughter. She couldn't believe how preposterous she looked, like some mythical hero. Even Quinn had been sculpted to look ridiculously magisterial.

'What is *that*?' she tittered. 'Is this what you wanted to show me?'

Clearly, this wasn't the reaction the leprechauns were hoping for. The proud smiles fell from their faces.

'Oh,' said Flannigan.

'You don't like it?' Seamus asked.

'Hmm,' Pat murmured sadly.

Bethany tried to control her laughter. 'No, no, I love it. It just . . . um, it caught me by surprise, that's all.'

The leprechauns all shrugged and made gestures as if they didn't care one way or another. They trudged away from the statue. 'We were passing this way anyway,' Flannigan said dismissively. 'Just thought you might want to see it. It's nothing really.'

'No, please,' Bethany insisted. 'It's really, really good. I'm just not used to being portrayed as a hero. I mean, I didn't really do anything special.'

This caused Flannigan to round on her. 'You stopped a major demonic event. And we made sure the Leprechaun High Council knew about that. Not just any old spirit has a statue made of them, you know.'

'I'm sorry,' Bethany said, sensing how badly she had upset them. 'I didn't realise.'

The sulking leprechauns walked away, turning down the end of the street. Bethany followed them round the corner and up the steps of the nearest building. It was the strange clockwork construction she had seen nestling at the heart of the city and it bustled with activity.

'Forget it,' Flannigan said. He was checking the ring on his finger. The gemstone was flashing a bright green. 'I just thought it might cheer you up before your meeting.'

'What do you mean?' Bethany asked. She noticed that the ring on her finger was also flashing and that the leprechauns were all looking up at the building with uneasy expressions. 'Flannigan, what is it? What is this place?'

'This is the justice building,' he said. 'You've been requested to give information on a criminal investigation.'

'Oh. Right.' She wasn't sure what to make of that. 'What's being investigated exactly?'

'Quinn,' came the reply.

CHAPTER FIVE

A NICE CUP OF TEA

The clockwork building had a bewildering array of halls, corridors and entrances involved in its intricate workings. Bethany and the leprechauns passed a hallway of doors that moved in synchronisation, like the sprockets of a revolving wheel. They ran up stairways that were the grooved edges of huge turning cogs, carrying them through a complicated mass of gears. There was an atmosphere of order and precision to the building that was impossible to ignore.

'I knew you were up to something,' she said angrily. 'You weren't coming to help me at all.'

'It's not our fault,' protested Flannigan.

'Look, whatever is going on, I don't want anything to do with it. OK? It's not my problem.'

'It really is too late for that,' he told her. They strode up a slanting corridor. The leprechauns here all wore black uniforms and had serious, grave faces. Flannigan came to a halt at a door as black and shiny as a beetle shell. The gemstone on his ring changed from a flashing light to a steady glow. 'This is it. Just try and be yourself,' he said.

The door swung open by itself. It revealed a long, spacious room with a formal appearance. There was a neat desk at the far end with a figure busily working away. He gestured for them to enter. Walls decorated with gemstones lit up as they stepped into the room. The hunched, knobbly figure rose from his seat and came forward to meet his guests. Hurm Igrig smiled in a pleasant and courteous manner. 'Well,' he said in mock surprise, 'this *is* a coincidence.'

'Yes,' Bethany replied, looking at the jowly, lumpy face and feeling a sense of deep foreboding. 'Isn't it?'

Hurm Igrig shook her hand and offered her a seat at the desk. The leprechauns, Bethany noticed, were already taking their place on a bench against the wall, reverting to the humble, obedient state they had adopted on the train. This put her on edge even more.

'A refreshment of some sort?' Hurm Igrig suggested.

'Um . . .' Bethany looked over her shoulder for guidance from Flannigan.

'I'm fond of this,' Hurm Igrig said in a disarmingly friendly way. He seemed like a different person to the rude and intimidating figure on the train. He clicked his fingers and two cups and saucers appeared on his desk. 'Cloud tea.'

He handed her a cup and she examined the contents. A perfectly formed miniature cloud hung over the steaming fluid. Tentatively, she sipped it. She had the strange sensation of raindrops pelting her tongue, as if she had opened her mouth in the middle of a rainstorm. It was, she had to admit, a peculiarly pleasant feeling that seemed to fill her spirit body with a warm glow of energy. She took several long sips.

'Leprechaun magic,' Hurm Igrig explained. He returned to his seat on the other side of the desk and took a large sip of tea. 'Hmmff. Very nice,' he murmured to himself. 'Now, to matters in hand . . .'

Bethany felt her nerves disappearing. The cloud tea seemed to have a calming effect on her.

Hurm Igrig's bushy eyebrows knitted together. He leaned forward. 'It is a privilege to meet you, Bethany Chase. I have heard all about your exploits.' He glanced briefly at Pat, Seamus and Flannigan. 'Very impressive indeed.'

'Um . . . thank you,' Bethany replied sheepishly.

'You and Quinn are legendary. Destroying that demon together . . . well, I cannot state my admiration enough. Creating a flaming sword out of pure magic – a masterful stroke. And using Quinn's mischievous aura to break down the demon's defensive spells – inspirational!'

Bethany opened her mouth to correct him. *What had Flannigan told him?* 'No, I —'

'How is your friend Quinn, by the way?' he asked her quickly before she had time to finish. 'Have you seen him recently?'

'I . . . yes, well, sort of . . . but . . .'

'Quite a team you made, yes?' he added. He chuckled to himself as if recalling some humorous part of their adventure, making a low *hmmff, hmmff, hmmff* noise.

'I suppose,' Bethany said. 'But it didn't really happen like you said. The thing with the demon.'

'No?' Hurm Igrig asked, becoming serious again. 'You didn't destroy a demon together?'

'We did, but . . . well, we thought we destroyed it, but it managed to escape. I saw it . . . in the spirit realm.' Bethany felt flustered. There was something intimidating about Hurm Igrig's presence that made her hesitant about telling him everything. His lumpy, misshapen face was completely unreadable and she couldn't decide whether he was being sincere or if he was feigning interest.

'You are not the slayer of demons?' the leprechaun asked.

'No . . . I mean, we sort of destroyed it. There was a hotel that was trapping spirits and we freed them but —'

The leprechaun held up his hand. 'Let me ask you something, Bethany Chase. Do you consider yourself to be friends with Quinn?'

'Well, yes. I suppose. Is he in trouble of some sort?' Bethany felt worried. 'Has something happened?'

If it was possible for Hurm Igrig's face to become more serious and sombre then it did so now. His bushy eyebrows formed one solid frown and his features hung heavier with an invisible weight. 'If he was in trouble of some sort, very *serious* trouble, would you help him,

Bethany Chase? Would you help your friend, Quinn?'

'I . . .' She felt unsure what he was asking, but she remembered how Quinn had helped her destroy the hotel and save her parents. He had helped her when no one else dared to. 'Of course I would,' she said decisively.

'Well, then,' Hurm Igrig said firmly. 'It is decided.'

Flannigan shifted in his seat. 'Sir, if I could just discuss this with Bethany for a moment?'

Hurm Igrig barely acknowledged him. 'You will be summoned to appear before the leprechaun court,' he instructed Bethany in an official tone.

She felt totally confused. 'I don't understand. What has Quinn done, exactly?'

Hurm Igrig took a large and satisfying sip of tea before replying. 'Quinn is responsible for the largest theft of leprechaun gold in our history,' he explained in a grave tone. He sat forward. 'If you will allow me to show you.'

Reluctantly, Bethany nodded her head.

There was a neat line of rings on the desk in front of Hurm Igrig, each with a different-coloured gemstone. He plucked out a ring encrusted with a bright red ruby and fitted it into a tall stand on his desk, a piece of equipment that looked like a long rod with a glowing tip. Light sprayed from the jewelled ring as it was fitted into place. A huge sphere of light shimmered with colours and blurry shapes, gradually resolving into familiar images. The pictures were in three dimensions, consisting of ghostly light and miniaturised to fit in a large area of space.

'This was retrieved from one of our officers.'

At the centre of the sphere was the officer wearing the ring. His image projected from the piece of jewellery in a bright light, clearer than the other figures. Surrounding him was a scene of complete chaos. Bethany recognised the Mineral Underground platform they had arrived at, though now she was looking at a platform that had been ripped apart and reduced to rubble by the effect of several explosions. A group of leprechauns in blue uniforms, including the officer with the ring, were battling against a single figure. That figure was Quinn and he was standing on board the train beside a stack of pots glowing with golden light.

A stream of sparks erupted from his right hand and struck several of the leprechauns. One was hit in the arm by the crackling beam of light and he convulsed as his limb began to shake. It burst open like exploding popcorn and loads of arms shot outwards from the area – small ones, chubby ones, thin ones, old ones. There were so many that the leprechaun overbalanced and fell to the ground. Beside him, his colleague had been hit in the foot and a cluster of odd-shaped feet had exploded along one leg.

'A simple abundance spell, as you can see,' commented Hurm Igrig. 'But used to devastating effect.'

The leprechauns in blue uniforms tried to retaliate with their own magic, but the best they could manage was a defensive spell that deflected Quinn's attacks and caused violent explosions to tear the station apart. Quinn was finding all of this immensely good fun as bolts of energy shot out of his fingertips in a sustained attack. His power was vast compared to the officers attempting to halt him, and Bethany could see why: he had one hand immersed in a golden pot and he was channelling the energy from it through his body.

'Quinn?' Bethany found herself saying in surprise.

At that moment, the officer who was wearing the ring tried to edge closer to the pooka. Quinn caught sight of him, however, and aimed a blast of magic at him. The leprechaun was engulfed in blue flames, causing the entire recording to fizzle and crackle. The officer fell backwards, clawing at his face. He had received a direct hit to the mouth and his chin suddenly bubbled outwards with a mass of lips. Quinn could be seen at the edges of the sphere, becoming steadily fainter as he escaped on the Mineral Underground. The recording stopped, halting with the image of the many-lipped officer unconscious on the ground.

'These are the last images we have of Quinn. We believe he has gone on the run and taken the gold into the physical realm, where it is harder for us to reach him.' Hurm Igrig tutted and harrumphed to himself. He shook his head sadly. 'He may be a spirit of mischief, but this is mischief on an unprecedented scale. The amount of gold he has stolen is sizeable, making him not only dangerous but extremely powerful.'

'But why did he do this?' Bethany asked, shocked, trying

to make sense of what she had just seen. She swivelled in her chair to get some response from Flannigan, but the leprechaun had his head bowed and was lost in deep thought, as if he too was contemplating Quinn's motives. Quinn was a trickster spirit, after all, but he had never been malicious like this.

'Why indeed?' Hurm Igrig replied in a tone of accusation. 'I'm sure only those close to him could have any idea.'

'Wait,' Bethany said. She dropped her cup of cloud tea down on the desk as it suddenly dawned on her what he was implying. 'You think I had something to do with this?'

'I'm saying nothing of the kind, I can assure you,' the leprechaun told her with an insincere smile.

Bethany persisted. 'But you think I helped him, don't you? That's what all of this is about.' She felt her spirit body tightening, as if her heart was hammering in her chest.

Hurm Igrig held his hands upwards in an innocent gesture. 'Please. This is just a preliminary investigation. You will have your chance to speak at the trial. I'm sorry if I have upset you in any way.'

This infuriated Bethany further. She fumed to herself, feeling tricked, lied to and manipulated. Flannigan appeared by her side, helping her up from her seat. The interview was clearly over.

'Thank you for agreeing to this meeting, young lady. It has been a privilege to meet you in person. It really has.' Hurm Igrig walked round his desk to say farewell to his guests, but Bethany was too angry to shake his hand. Instead, she stormed off towards the door, muttering to herself. Flannigan fluttered around Hurm Igrig, making excuses for her.

'She's very tired, sir. It's an effect of the transmigration. We really look forward to seeing you at the trial, sir. A real honour.'

Hurm Igrig grumbled and spluttered, giving the impression he was offended by some aspect of Bethany's behaviour. This only made her more angry. By the time Flannigan, Pat and Seamus had caught up with her at the doorway her fury was ready to burst. She turned on her heels and pointed a finger at Hurm Igrig. He was sitting back down at his desk and examining a ring with a small blue gem.

'I think you are an extremely rude and —' But Flannigan slapped his hand over her mouth and the leprechauns yanked her through the open door before she could share her views about Hurm Igrig. Flannigan tried to sound offhand and cheerful.

'Bye now,' he called.

He pulled the door closed and the leprechauns hurried down the corridor, Pat and Seamus lugging the pot behind them. When they were far enough down the corridor, Flannigan released his hand from Bethany's mouth and gave her a stern, disapproving look. 'Well, that didn't go very well, did it?'

'DON'T YOU DARE!' Bethany shrieked at him. The

leprechauns visibly shrivelled at her tone of fury and all three took a step back. 'Why didn't you tell me that was going to happen, Flannigan? Quinn stealing gold? Me being accused of helping him? That was horrible! What is going on here?'

'I don't think he was accusing you as such.' Flannigan tried to reason with her, but quickly thought better of it as she glared at him threateningly. 'I'm sorry. I thought it would be better if you didn't know anything, that it would make you look more innocent. Hurm Igrig is one of the best investigators there is. He can sniff out a lie at a hundred paces.' He sighed and threw up his arms. 'I didn't think it would go so badly.'

'Well, it did,' Bethany snapped. She walked away, bristling with anger.

'There is nothing more to be done about it until the trial,' Flannigan told her sternly. 'That is that.'

The four of them moved through the justice building in a gloomy silence, passing oversized pendulums, turning dials and clicking gears. On the steps outside, Bethany found herself staring out at the bizarre buildings of the magical city once more: an austere, tall construction made from ice, a floating silvery spire anchored by a thick chain, and a huge hexagonal structure made from large slabs of stone covered in gold.

Flannigan caught her looking at them. He pointed at the large hexagonal building. 'That was what the pyramids could have been like,' he said casually.

Bethany wanted to stay in a bad mood with him for the

trouble he had caused her, but she was too fascinated to let the comment go. 'What do you mean that could have been the pyramids? That's the stupidest thing I've ever heard.'

'Well. That was the original idea for the pyramids before we stole it. It's like I said, our gold turns into many things, things that shape your world in profound ways.'

'So you're telling me you stole an entire building?'

'No, no,' he laughed. 'This is the spirit realm. These buildings are just ideas. We stole the idea and changed the future. See, before anything exists it starts out as a possibility, and that possibility is pure magic – it's our gold. The city is full of it.'

'Full of gold you stole,' Bethany added.

The leprechauns did not see anything wrong with this and actually seemed proud of it. 'Exactly right. That's why we call it the Stolen City,' Flannigan told her. 'Here, I'll show you before we take you home. It might cheer you up.'

Reluctantly, Bethany followed as he walked to the doors of a nearby building. They passed several groups of leprechauns wearing coloured uniforms. There were three female leprechauns in brown outfits who had wide curious faces, and beside them was a huddle of smaller spirits in red uniforms who had long jutting chins and slightly snide grins. She tried not to react as they stared at her and whispered among themselves. All of them, she noticed, wore a chunky jewelled ring on their finger, and she was about to ask Flannigan how the rings worked when they reached a wide arched entrance.

'See?' he said, pointing inside.

Bethany peered in. There was a vast interior full of sprouting plants that were stacked up in row after row of oversized shelves. It looked like a plush and extremely unlikely forest, with all types of flowers and trees and bushes that Bethany had never seen before. Nearest to her was a bright blue cactus as tall as a full-sized man, then a polka-dot flower in the shape of an upturned umbrella, and along from it was something that looked like a tree growing sideways.

'This is the building of plants-that-never-were. It is full of every plant that never existed. Imagine a world full of sticky eggtrees, or the huge blue scroob, or the cackling moss.'

'Hmm. Imagine,' Bethany said, intrigued.

Flannigan nodded in agreement. 'That's right. It would be unthinkable.'

He led her away from the building, striding quickly down the street. Bethany glanced at the buildings with renewed interest. 'So each of these is full of similar things?'

The leprechauns nodded. 'Ideas, possibilities, potentials,' Flannigan boasted. 'Over there is the building of animals-that-could-have-been. And beside it is the place of lost inventions. Then there is the home of stolen songs.'

She tried to estimate how many buildings there were.

'For every interesting thing that exists, be it a plant, an invention, a piece of music, there are hundreds of similar things that never made it. Things that we stole.'

'Really?' Bethany said, suddenly brightening. She ran

over to a large vault-like door. 'Can I have a look?'

The leprechauns rushed after her. Briefly, she glimpsed a bizarre zoo full of strange creatures. Something with hairy tentacles and glistening eyes glowered back at her before Seamus caught her and marched her away. She bolted free, though, and made it across to the next building.

'It probably isn't for the best,' Seamus suggested. 'You know, under the circumstances.'

'What circumstances?' she called back at him. She made it to the entrance of a tiny building, no bigger than a shack. Inside, however, was a stadium-sized interior that stretched up as far as the eye could see. There were thousands of ladders of different heights reaching up to mysterious black holes that hung in the air. Leprechauns in yellow uniforms were scampering up and down the ladders, carrying glowing pots and disappearing through the holes.

Seamus and Flannigan marched her away before she could see any more. Although Pat, she noticed, was allowed to run into the building, dragging his pot after him. 'That's not fair,' she complained.

'That's the place of lost inventions. It's top-level security. It's extremely risky for you to be near it,' Flannigan said sternly. 'You're a human. If you even caught a glimpse of an invention it could change the course of history for ever.'

'But Pat —'

'Is depositing our catch.' They bundled her away. 'We need to be going.'

'Back home?' she asked hopefully.

Flannigan nodded.

They made it back to their walking chairs and started on their return journey to the station. Galloping after them, Pat soon caught up, and it wasn't long before all four of them were back on the Mineral Underground, holding on to the diamonds as the train shot upwards.

They sat in silence for most of the journey. Bethany had too much to think about to talk. The carriage moved through the crystal tunnels, dense underground layers, and finally the foundations of London they had passed through on their previous journey. Judging by the pale sky, they had arrived shortly before dawn, and the train carried out its erratic journey of twists and turns.

Bethany finally spoke up. 'I was wondering. What was Quinn doing in your city before he stole all the gold?'

Flannigan seemed lost in his thoughts, as he had been in Hurm Igrig's office. Seamus answered for him. 'Working.'

'Really? What as?'

Seamus looked at Flannigan as if he should check what to say, then shrugged. 'He had been given honorary status. You know, after you had both been hailed as heroes for destroying the Jackomuss demon, he was given the job of chief demon hunter.'

Bethany frowned. 'Demon hunter?' she echoed.

Without any warning, the train skidded in a wide arc and came to an abrupt halt. She peeked out of the window and saw the huge bedroom window of her aunt's house. A bell sounded *ding-ding* and the doors opened. Flannigan came out of his thoughts and they all hurried on to the windowsill, where Bethany was confronted with the peculiar sight of her own body, as tall in size to her as a giant, grinning down at her and saying, 'You took your time.'

The leprechauns moved quickly to return Bethany to her proper size and put her back into her body. Hurrying inside, Pat and Seamus placed their pot carefully into position and threw her into it. She felt a flash of golden light surge through her and her spirit body exploded outwards, hurtling forwards and expanding at the same time. There was an unpleasant feeling of connecting with something heavy and solid, followed by a sense of relief as she glanced down at herself, back in her body where she should be.

She looked at the reassuringly solid walls, solid bed and solid window. Faintly, she could make out the leprechauns hurrying across the duvet and clambering on to the windowsill. Donovan was leaping about excitedly and he swung round to wave at her. 'It's been a nice week,' he laughed. 'And I didn't break anything. Honest.'

Week? she thought. *What is he talking about?*

Flannigan was the last to get on the train. He looked sheepish. 'Ah, now. I forgot to mention the time dissonance. Just try and eat lots and don't overexert yourself.' He became more serious. 'We'll be back to get you soon. Whatever you do, avoid Quinn. Prolonged exposure to that much leprechaun gold can have terrible side-effects out here in the physical realm – madness and such. As for this cat you mentioned, keep away from that as well, especially if it starts to behave in an unusual manner. It's extremely important for the case.' His voice rose in urgency. 'Don't do anything remotely risky or dangerous. *And stay at home as much as possible.* Understood?'

Bethany nodded her head.

The train doors closed on Flannigan and she watched the faint blur of motion zigzagging through the sky as the Mineral Underground rushed to its next stop. It was all too much to take in. She was back in her body, at least, but she couldn't help worrying that Donovan hadn't looked after it properly while she'd been away. After all, it wasn't like lending someone a pair of trainers or a jacket. Her exhausted mind reeled at the shift in states. She tried to make sense of the bizarre journey she had just been on, but it seemed a very good idea at that moment to go to sleep.

CHAPTER SIX

A RISING TREND

Normality, it turned out, felt extremely strange. It took Bethany the entire morning to adjust. Her body felt large and cumbersome. Objects seemed unnaturally heavy. Her mind had a dazed quality, as if she had woken from a particularly vivid dream. She was roused from sleep by her alarm clock. Donovan must have set it, though, as it was far earlier than her usual waking time, and Bethany switched it off and snoozed for another hour until she was ready to get up. She dragged herself out of bed and groggily made her way downstairs. The cats and dogs, perhaps sensing her mood, left her alone when she eventually wandered into the kitchen for her breakfast.

Mr and Mrs Chase were already up but there was no sign

of Aunt Bess. 'Morning!' Mrs Chase said as soon as she saw Bethany.

'Just in time for toast,' her father announced, removing several slices from the toaster. He was dressed smartly in a shirt and tie and was pushing the cats away from him with more force than usual. 'Keep *off*, I don't want to look like a furball today, thanks all the same.'

Bethany took a seat at the table beside her mother, who was browsing the morning newspaper.

'You're up late today,' Mrs Chase remarked.

'Am I?' Bethany replied sleepily. Her father placed the plate of toast on to the table. 'What's the occasion?' she asked him.

Her mother shot her a disapproving look. '*Bethany*, it's your father's interview today. You've not forgotten, have you?'

'Um . . . no, course not,' she said, feeling confused. Her father made some jokey comment to her, then her mother spoke, but she wasn't really registering what they were saying. Instead, she was thinking that she should have found out from Donovan what had been happening while she'd been away. She greedily grabbed several slices of toast and smothered them in jam before noisily munching her way through them. She felt famished and wondered if that was a side-effect of transmigration. 'Sorry, what did you say?' she asked as her mother repeated a question.

'I said, what time do you want to go to the museum?' Mrs Chase asked loudly.

'Museum? . . . Um, I don't know. Are we going to a museum today?'

Mrs Chase groaned with exasperation. '*You* were the one who wanted to go, young lady. Are you telling me after days of going on about it you don't want to bother now?'

Bethany felt uneasy as she looked up at her mother and noticed the newspaper for the first time. There was a small picture of Quinn on the front page. She snatched the paper without thinking and gawped at the image of Quinn's grinning head.

'Bethany!' Mrs Chase exclaimed.

'I don't know what has got into you,' Mr Chase said in a frustrated tone. He took the newspaper out of her hands and returned it to Bethany's mother. 'But we do not grab the newspaper when someone else is reading it. Understood?'

'Yeah . . . sorry,' she murmured. But Bethany had just noticed something else alarming. 'It's the fifteenth,' she said, reading the date. She looked up at her parents, expecting them to be as shocked by this realisation as she was. Instead, they stared back at her with bewildered expressions. 'The fifteenth! That means an entire week has passed.' What was worse, Donovan must have been impersonating her all that time. She couldn't help picturing herself being controlled by him, excitedly running around London, probably asking all sorts of ridiculous questions and, all in all, generally behaving in a completely odd manner. She was sure she could sense it in her body, as if the leprechaun had left a trace of himself behind. *This was turning into a nightmare.*

She groaned loudly. Worst of all, it seemed her own family had barely even noticed.

Her parents both glared at her. 'Honestly, what has come over you?' her mother asked. She had a baffled expression and it took Bethany a few moments to realise how strange she must be acting.

'Oh, nothing, I'm just . . . tired. I didn't sleep well,' she said, trying to appear as normal as possible. 'And the museum thing. How could I forget? I'm really, really, really excited about it. I'm just going to get ready now. Just get a few . . . museum things together. Good luck with the interview, Dad.'

She obviously hadn't convinced them that she was normal as they both wore puzzled expressions. Luckily, Aunt Bess entered the room at that moment, singing away to herself, and Bethany escaped upstairs. She ran into her bedroom and sat on the edge of the bed, thoughts racing. *A week! That was what Flannigan must have meant when he mentioned the time dissonance. Why hadn't they warned her of that in the first place?*

She tried not to think about the leprechauns or their city but it wasn't easy. She could feel the ring on her finger that Flannigan had given her, although when she looked directly at her hand there was nothing to be seen. This bothered her and she decided it was best to concentrate on getting ready rather than try to make sense of an invisible ring. She found that she was still clumsy, knocking things over and stumbling into the piles of boxes. Several times she checked the window for any signs of the sinister cat, but mercifully, it was not there.

Mrs Chase was patiently waiting for Bethany at the

bottom of the stairs. 'I swear, you are a mystery to me. One minute you're lost in a book, then you're full of energy, now you're dragging your feet. Talk about running hot and cold.'

Bethany uttered a loud, false laugh. 'You know me, always different from one day to the next.'

'So it would seem,' Mrs Chase agreed with a wry smile.

They managed to squeeze through the pack of excited animals and out the front door. They had barely made it to the end of the street when Bethany noticed a huge picture of Quinn. His grinning, slightly demented face stared back from an advert on the side of a bus shelter. Beneath it was the simple caption: QUINN – *BELIEVE*.

'What is going on?' Bethany muttered to herself as she set eyes on it. She giggled in a bemused fashion. It was strange seeing him like this, not entirely real, as if she hadn't fully woken yet.

Her mother looked quizzically from Bethany to the poster, then rolled her eyes. 'Please don't start going on about Quinn again. I don't know what all the fuss is about.'

'What? Have I . . . have I been going on about Quinn lots?'

'No, no. Only every time you see that poster,' her mother replied sarcastically.

'Oh, yeah. *That* poster.'

Mrs Chase sighed. 'I mean, at least in our day our celebrities were famous for something.'

Bethany tried to think of a reply but she was distracted by two boys walking past them on the pavement. They looked like a double act, one exceedingly tall and gangly, the other short and broad, and both wearing similar red tracksuit tops. They were daring each other to eat the contents from a colourful packet of sweets. With each mouthful, their faces contorted and a series of colourful sparks and flashes burst from their mouths. They laughed at the effects of the strange fizzing, crackling powder. That packet, Bethany saw, was emblazoned with a logo of Quinn's grinning face.

Remain calm, Bethany told herself, even though she felt far from calm. Her bemusement turned abruptly to concern. *What happened while I was away?* She had an overriding urge to run back to the house and try to find out something about Quinn on the internet, but she knew she couldn't behave any more strangely in front of her mother.

They walked towards the nearest tube station and took the train to central London. Several times she caught glimpses of the same mischievous face, the same dollop of pink hair and the same impossibly wide grin. It was on billboards in stations, on adverts on the back of magazines, and it was even on the discarded packets of sweet wrappers dropped on the ground by her feet. By the time they reached the museum she had seen his likeness loads of times.

All Bethany could think was that it was one of his mischievous tricks, although on a massive scale. She knew that there was always an honourable motive behind his seemingly random behaviour. But she wondered what he was doing now. *Was there something the leprechauns weren't telling her? Was there something they were hiding?* She had seen the images of him stealing the gold, but had been shown nothing before or after that might explain his reasons for the theft, and she hadn't trusted Hurm Igrig at all. *If there was only some way of contacting him directly*, she thought. She groaned at the realisation that she was being dragged into events whether she wanted to be or not.

'Are you sure you're all right?' Mrs Chase asked. 'You appear to be groaning more than usual.'

'Sorry,' Bethany said without thinking. 'It's just . . . tiredness.'

An excited Japanese tourist was standing at the entrance to the museum, having his photo taken as he held a red balloon with Quinn's face painted on it. It was enough to push Bethany over the edge.

'What does he think he's doing?' Bethany said loudly, shaking her head.

Her mother, thinking that Bethany was talking about the Japanese tourist, snapped at her. 'Behave! Right this minute.'

'But . . .' She tried to think of a way to explain what was happening.

'Now, I know things have not been easy for you and that you wanted to spend the summer in Stagtree Knoll, but . . . we've all had to make sacrifices, Bethany.'

'It's not that, Mum,' Bethany insisted.

Her mother wasn't listening, though. 'We are trying our hardest, you know. It is a difficult time for both your father and me. It doesn't help when you keep behaving in this odd manner of yours. So please, can we attempt to have a normal day together?'

Bethany listened intently and solemnly. She would have found it easier to agree with her mother if she hadn't just glimpsed a black cat perched by the railings, peering at her with its piercing orange eyes.

Remain really calm, she told herself. She looked back at her mother, trying to act as unfazed as possible. 'Of course. Normality's my middle name,' she said.

Mrs Chase sighed with relief. 'Good. Now let's go and enjoy this exhibition of . . .' She checked the guide in her hand. 'Precious and semi-precious gemstones. Hmmm. Well, we can at least try.'

As Bethany looked over her mother's shoulder, another strange sight greeted her. A bus trundled by with a huge picture of Quinn painted on one side. The vehicle stopped at a set of traffic lights and the giant grinning face winked at her once – or so she imagined – before the bus pulled off. The black cat mewled and hissed, then it faced Bethany and sneezed at her three times, very precisely.

'No you don't,' Bethany muttered under her breath. She felt a tingling sensation from her ring and took a step towards the animal. She was distracted by a loud BANG! by her shoulder. The balloon that the Japanese tourist had been holding burst so loudly that the flock of pigeons at his feet took to the air in a single mass movement, causing everyone outside the museum to look up suddenly in the same direction. This in turn caused a passing cyclist to turn and look, which was unfortunate as he was veering into the path of an oncoming car.

'Watch out!' Bethany shouted, too late.

The cyclist slammed on his brakes and the car swerved out of the way to avoid a collision, mounting the pavement and crashing into the set of metal railings with enough force to crumple the bonnet and set off airbags inside the vehicle. Everybody froze with shock. The car had missed Bethany by a few inches.

Quietly, the black cat slunk away, its long curly tail bobbing from side to side.

'Are you sure you're all right?' Mrs Chase asked for the seventh or eighth time.

'I'm fine,' Bethany reassured her, although in truth she was shaken far more than she was willing to let on. There was no doubt now. The cat was trying to kill her – and she needed to find out why.

Luckily, no one had been hurt in the accident, but the driver was furious about the damage to his car. A heated argument broke out between him and the cyclist over whose fault it had been and Mrs Chase had to give a statement to the police. Bethany, meanwhile, waited nervously by the museum entrance, constantly checking to see if the black cat was anywhere to be seen. Her mind raced with ideas and suspicions. She didn't know why the cat was attacking her, but she was certain Quinn had intervened just in time. She might not be as lucky if there was another encounter.

Mrs Chase and Bethany both pretended to forget about the accident as they ambled through the museum, staring at the glass cabinets full with displays of gemstones and jewels. It was a welcome relief from the chaos outside and Bethany could see why Donovan would have wanted to come here. The chunks of cloudy crystals and the glittering speckled stones made her think of the Stolen City, but that only made her wonder when the leprechauns would be back for her, which was a distinctly depressing thought.

Mrs Chase, in an effort to appear interested, kept reading the descriptions of stones out loud, then making a surprised noise as if she was fascinated to discover a new fact. 'Lapis lazuli was used as the blue pigment for the paintings of the Renaissance. Well . . . I didn't know that. And look, obsidian is formed from magma. Hmmm. Interesting.' She sounded thoroughly unconvinced. It was as if each was pretending to enjoy it for the other's benefit, and they were both glad to finally leave when they ran out of exhibits.

The journey home was unnecessarily cautious as they carefully crossed roads and halted at any sudden noises, Mrs Case being overly protective of her daughter. As they walked along a busy main street towards the tube station an odd sight greeted them. Children of all ages were gathering around a newsagent's, running out of the shop with pink and yellow packets clutched in their hands. Groups of them were standing on the pavement, comparing the effects of the sweets. Their mouths crackled and popped with colourful sparks, while others were having their faces comically stretched. This was creating a great deal of hilarity and excitement.

'How peculiar,' Mrs Chase remarked.

Bethany approached the nearest group. A boy her own age with spiky black hair and a green camouflage T-shirt was trying out one of the sweets. As he chewed his face carried out a series of bizarre contortions. It was as if his features were made of rubber and someone was stretching and squishing them in quick succession to produce a series of funny and ugly faces. When it finally stopped, the boy wore a brief, dazed expression before announcing, 'Brilliant!' He chuckled to himself.

'What is *that*?' she asked, giggling at the sight of so many kids having their faces stretched, or their mouths seemingly exploding with fireworks, or gasping at something they had just seen in the chocolate bars they were chomping. She knew, of course, before she heard the answer what the cause of so much outrageous fun was.

'Quinn's,' the boy declared, waving the tube at her. 'Here, try one.'

Bethany examined the packet. The sweets were called 'Facetoffees' and bore a colourful pink and yellow wrapper with Quinn's face on the front. She took one and cautiously put it in her mouth. Initially, it tasted no different to a normal toffee, but as soon as it started to soften and she began chewing it, something peculiar happened. When she bit down on the toffee, her entire face squashed down. As soon as the toffee stretched between her teeth her face also stretched lengthways. And the faster she chewed the faster and more violently her face contorted. The effect was

83

obviously as funny to look at as it was to experience, since Mrs Chase erupted into squeals and snorts of laughter at her daughter's expressions.

'Are you sure you're enjoying that?' Mrs Chase asked, chortling.

Bethany tried to reply, but all that came out was a series of groans and burbles. Only once the toffee had dissolved could she speak again. 'That,' she said, 'was weird!'

They both burst into a fit of laughter.

'We should buy some,' Bethany suggested, imagining what some of the other sweets might do.

'It does seem like fun,' her mother admitted, grinning, glad to see her daughter enjoying herself.

It wasn't until Bethany turned round and saw how many people were doing the same thing, consuming the curious sweets and falling about in fits of laughter, that she realised how strange the whole thing was. The entire street, it seemed, had collapsed in hysterics, and it gave the eerie impression that everybody had momentarily lost their minds. *He's using the magic*, she realised. *He's using the magic in the sweets. There's no other explanation for it.* Her heart lurched. *Why here, like this?*

'Actually, maybe we should go back home now,' Bethany said, her mood shifting.

Mrs Chase threw her hands up in despair. 'Make your mind up.'

Bethany suddenly felt unsafe in the street, exposed. She thought of the cat and wondered if it might return if they lingered too long outside. Mostly, she considered the sweets. Quinn could not have created them with his own magic. It was too much for one pooka. That meant that he *had* stolen the gold, just as the leprechauns said, and he was using it.

CHAPTER SEVEN

THE
MIGHTY QUINN

Bethany scoured the internet for information about Quinn as soon as they made it back to the house. Just as she had thought, there were several web pages with his name mentioned. There were places you could order Quinn products. There were vague references to him in newspaper articles. There was even a discussion group full of questions and opinions about who he was, with comments ranging from a fan who thought he was a famous American actor who had received huge amounts of plastic surgery, to a person who thought he was based on a Japanese cartoon character. But for all her efforts, Bethany could find no actual information about him anywhere. Everything she found praised him or recommended his products without giving any concrete facts. It was infuriating. All she needed was some way to get in touch with him.

She retreated to her bedroom and tried to think about what she should do. It looked like Donovan had been busy protecting the room while she had been away. He had drawn strange symbols on to sheets of paper that he had stuck to the wall, which Bethany guessed were magical inscriptions. They certainly seemed to repel the cat – she caught glimpses of it prowling the neighbour's garden late at night, but it never dared to get nearer.

The mood in the house was subdued over the next few days. Mr Chase had not had a successful interview and Mrs Chase had upset Aunt Bess by insisting on vacuuming every day to keep the animal hair under control. Aunt Bess was obviously not used to spending her time with other people and seemed to focus her attention on the animals as a way of coping, feeding them several times a day and fussing over them. The animals, at least, were enjoying this, looking plump and contented.

Eventually, Bethany stopped sulking in her room and went out searching for answers. She wondered how far Quinn's influence was spreading. She snuck out and scouted the neighbourhood. It didn't take her long to find a shop selling Quinn products. It bustled with activity and she had to barge her way through several people to get her hands on some of the sweets. On the pavement outside she tested their effects. One was a chunky chocolate bar that had a picture of Quinn's face running through it like the lettering in a stick of rock, although with each bite the picture changed, as if it was a film being moved forward a frame at a time, so that the face winked then smiled then disappeared. It was a clever trick, she had to admit, and it made her smile.

Another packet contained Fizzbombs – *like fireworks for your mouth*, the packet declared – and she was startled when she tried a mouthful of the gritty powder. Flavours exploded from her tongue in a spray of colourful sparks. She could taste intense bursts of orange and lemon as the powder fizzled and crackled. It did indeed feel like a firework was going off in her mouth, yet there was no heat, just a bright cascade of flavours.

As funny as she found this, she couldn't shake the feeling that there was something off-putting about the sweets. Maybe it was due to the fact that she knew magic was involved, or maybe it was because she knew Quinn liked to play tricks, but she dumped the remains in a nearby bin and decided to avoid the pink and yellow packets.

Each day she noticed a new facet of Quinn's fame and popularity. There was the version of his grinning face that had been made into a logo that she noticed on badges and T-shirts. The other version of his face appeared on magazines, on TV and the internet. This was Quinn in human form, like an extremely jolly fat man, dressed in a black bodysuit, a slightly crazed expression in his eyes and pink hair that resembled candyfloss.

At least newspapers were passing comment on this

strange trend, although Bethany was surprised at the excited tone of these articles. *Who is this mysterious character?* one tagline read. *What a breath of fresh air!* another announced. *Whoever he is, I'm a believer,* commented a third. There was even a picture of a normally earnest journalist enjoying a Facetoffee. This made Bethany chuckle to herself. *If only they knew who Quinn really was.*

Other Quinn products began to appear in the supermarket. The pink and yellow packaging was instantly recognisable. There was Quinn brand toothpaste *for that extra wide smile* and Quinn brand perfume and aftershaves *for the i-Stink generation.* There was a whole range of beauty and grooming products, from lipsticks to hair dyes. It all seemed so ludicrous to Bethany, much more so than the sweets, that she was certain it wouldn't catch on. But she was wrong – it didn't take long for these new trends to take root.

On a trip to the shops, she noticed a smartly dressed woman stepping out of a hairdresser's. The woman's hair had been styled into a pink quiff and she paused to admire it in a shop window before strolling off down the street. Moments later Bethany bumped into a broad man with thick glasses. She apologised and he smiled at her, his face stretching to accommodate the impossibly wide grin that gleamed with white teeth. Bethany did a double take, thinking for a brief moment that she had knocked into Quinn, so familiar was that smile. Next, in the street outside her aunt's house she saw the two boys whom she had first noticed eating the firework sweets, although instead of their identical tracksuits they were now wearing black bodysuits like the one Quinn wore in all the adverts.

This is too weird, Bethany thought as she sprinted into the house. She was sure that Quinn must have been intending this whole thing as an elaborate joke, but she couldn't laugh any more. *Everybody looked ridiculous. How could they not notice?* He was involving too many innocent people in his mischief, and he was taking it too far. She remembered what Flannigan had said, that prolonged exposure to the leprechaun gold could cause madness. *Has it twisted Quinn's judgement?* she wondered.

As usual, the animals rushed at her as soon as she was indoors. Bethany was glad of the attention. She played with them for a short while, throwing a mangled rubber toy for the dogs to fetch, then dangling string for the cats to claw at. She could hear her mother and Aunt Bess upstairs in the bathroom.

'Well, what does it say on the back?' Mrs Chase asked.

Aunt Bess cleared her throat loudly before replying. 'It just says to leave it on for five minutes, then rinse.'

'Well, is it five minutes yet?'

'Oh, am I keeping an eye on the time as well?' Aunt Bess said in a slightly sarcastic but otherwise friendly manner. 'I really don't see what was wrong with your hair in the first place.'

Bethany's ears pricked up. She dropped the scuffed dog toy and ran upstairs, peeking her head round the bathroom door. Her mother was sitting on a small stool by the bathtub with a red paste glueing her long brown hair down to her scalp. Aunt Bess was standing over her, wearing the polythene gloves she had used to apply the paste and checking her watch. Bethany burst in.

'No. Mum, don't do it! You don't need pink hair. Please.'

The two women looked at her.

'But it's not going to be pink, Bethany,' her mother said, slightly confused at the interruption.

'Oh, right . . .'

Aunt Bess tapped her watch. 'OK, that's five minutes now. Lean over the bath and I'll give you a good hose down.'

'I think you're beginning to enjoy this,' Mrs Chase complained.

Aunt Bess held Mrs Chase over the bathtub and aimed the showerhead over her hair, handling her in a brisk, forceful manner. 'It's much like washing down one of the dogs,' she quipped.

'Charmed, I'm sure.'

To Bethany's relief, her mother's hair was not pink but a dark, tawny red. The hair dye was, however, still one of Quinn's products – she could see the discarded box in the bin. 'Mum, why are you dyeing your hair?' Bethany asked. Her mother had, for as long as she could remember, always had the same hair style.

'It was supposed to be a surprise,' Mrs Chase said, drying her hair with a towel and checking the results in the bathroom mirror. 'They were half price. They're doing some promotion thingy where there's a lucky ticket in one of the packets. I think you win a day out or something. Anyway, I thought I would treat myself. What do you think?'

Bethany tried to make appreciative noises as her mother showed off her hair. 'It's really . . . interesting. I mean, it's nice and everything, but what was wrong with your hair the way it was?'

Her mother shrugged her shoulders and wrinkled her nose. 'Well, I needed to cheer myself up, try something different. Look . . .' She took her handbag from behind the door and scrabbled around in it until she found a yellow and pink flyer. She thrust it at Bethany. 'I thought you would be interested in this. They were handing them out at the supermarket.'

The piece of paper showed the obligatory picture of Quinn's grinning face. The writing beneath it read, *QUINN – A UNIQUE PUBLIC APPEARANCE. FREE GIFTS! FREE GIVEAWAYS! THIS SATURDAY AT 2 P.M.*

'Saturday? But that's tomorrow,' Bethany said. She could hardly believe it. *A chance to meet Quinn in the flesh! This was perfect. This was exactly what she needed.* 'He's going to be at the supermarket tomorrow? Can we go?'

'Of course we can go.' Mrs Chase giggled as she fluffed up her hair.

Aunt Bess peered over Bethany's shoulder at the picture of Quinn. 'What a strange-looking man. What does he do?'

'Do?' Mrs Chase echoed. 'He works miracles, that's what he does.'

Her hair did indeed have a brilliant red hue to it. Maybe

that was why it was so eye-catching and why Mrs Chase was dancing around in front of the mirror admiring it. Bethany and Aunt Bess shared a sideways glance. 'Miracle worker indeed,' Aunt Bess muttered.

Nevertheless, Bethany couldn't help feeling excited. She had not seen Quinn in person for a year and she began to feel nervous about seeing him again. *Maybe he would not be as friendly as he once had been. Maybe he had changed.* Part of her kept recalling the images she had seen of Quinn stealing the gold and injuring the leprechauns with magic. It made her realise that she needed questions to ask him. She found a scrap of paper and started scribbling down ideas.

Why did you steal the gold?
Why are you using it to become famous in the physical realm?
Why is the cat trying to hurt me?
What did your demon hunter job involve?
Are the leprechauns trying to hide something?

Bethany stared at the list and contemplated the questions. Her only worry was that Quinn was extremely elusive and it would be an achievement to get any sort of answer out of him. For a start, he never spoke. And even if he wrote the answers down it was still a lot to expect him to explain to her. She reconsidered, scoring out everything she had written and replacing it with a single sentence.

What is going on?

It was extremely important that he answer this question if she hoped to get his help or find out what was happening. The leprechauns could return at any time to take her back to the Stolen City to give evidence in the trial against Quinn. What then? Somehow she had to persuade Quinn to go back with her and sort out the whole mess himself. And return the gold. And stop making his strange products. And stop appearing in the physical realm. And . . .

That night Bethany barely slept. She was up early in the morning, making sure she was ready. Her mother was similarly enthusiastic, if only for the opportunity to show off her hair. Mr Chase decided to join them, although he seemed preoccupied and distant, having been unsuccessful with several more interviews that week. Aunt Bess was reluctant to come and Bethany didn't want to pester her, so she dragged her parents out of the door as soon as breakfast was finished.

'This is exciting!' Mrs Chase enthused.

'Well, it's free,' grumbled Mr Chase. 'That's something, I suppose.'

'We might even win some Quinn products,' Mrs Chase added.

Bethany didn't care about that. She just needed to get close enough to Quinn to be able to get his attention and speak to him. He would recognise her, she was sure, but she had to make sure she was at the front, in plain view. She hurried so that they would be some of the first people there, but was dismayed to see a small crowd had already gathered in the supermarket car park when they arrived, waiting behind a line of metal railings. Half the group consisted of

Quinn fans – people with dyed pink hair, or stretched smiles, or Quinn clothes. The other half was made up of curious bystanders, wondering what all the fuss was about.

'We need to get to the front,' Bethany told her parents, dragging them towards the group.

'Careful there,' said a bearded man with a small boy perched on his shoulders.

Several people tutted. A woman in a rainbow-coloured jumper and a shock of pink running though her long hair wagged her finger at Bethany. 'There are other people here beside yourself, young lady.'

'But . . .' Bethany felt like saying that she knew Quinn, but realised that no one would believe her.

'This is a good spot,' her father assured her. They were standing behind a particularly tall couple chatting to their particularly wide friend.

Bethany sighed and shifted from foot to foot impatiently. Her finger tingled where she felt the invisible ring was. It had tingled when the black cat had appeared outside the museum, and she kept a lookout among the legs of the surrounding crowd, expecting to see two orange eyes peering back at her. The thought made her nervous.

The sense of excitement mounted as a large white van pulled up in front of the metal barriers. A group of people emerged from the vehicle, wearing Quinn-style clothes, with pink quiffs, wide grins and strangely smooth heads. They began flinging goodie bags into the crowd, as well as handing out pink and yellow flags with Quinn's face on.

This caused excited yells and laughter as people caught the freebies. Mr Chase leaped up and snatched a bag as it flew over his head. He let out a great belly laugh.

'Now, this is my sort of day out,' he announced cheerily. 'Free stuff.'

'Free stuff to share,' Mrs Chase corrected, already inspecting the contents of the bag and squealing with delight.

Bethany looked behind her as the merchandise was distributed to the crowd. The group was increasing in size as more people arrived, drawn by the cheers. She could feel her anxiety increasing. *Maybe he's not coming after all, it's just a way of getting people here.*

A ripple of anticipation passed through the waiting group at that moment. A limousine slowly approached the front of the supermarket. A press photographer stirred into action, aiming his camera at the car's tinted windows, and fans called out Quinn's name. Bethany checked all the adults surrounding her and picked her moment carefully. 'Back soon,' she told her parents. She let go of her father's hand and ducked down low, swiftly forcing her way through to the front.

'Bethany, where do you think you're going?' she heard her father call after her in a worried tone.

People moved out of her way as she barged to the front. She was just in time to see the limousine pass slowly by. The passenger window lowered several inches and a shape moved inside the car, examining the faces of the expectant crowd.

'QUINN!' Bethany screeched as loudly as she could, waving her hands. Her voice was joined by a chorus of cries from fans eager to attract his attention. Everyone was desperate to get a glimpse of him and people swayed forward. There was a brief flicker of movement from the back seat. As if on command, the limousine came to a halt and a hush settled over the crowd.

Nobody dared move as a face appeared at the open window. It was a very strange-looking face, very round and smooth with a disproportionately large grin with teeth as big as piano keys, a tiny upturned nose, lumpy ears and two eyes that glinted with a wild mischief. The face seemed to glow with its own unique light. Everybody felt compelled to look at it, and the effect was so powerful that for several moments the entire car park was completely silent as people stopped and stared with amazement. As Bethany looked at him she could feel a peculiar mixture of awe and adoration so strong she was sure it had to be an effect created by the magic he had stolen.

It was enough to snap her out of her trance. Before anyone else had a chance to speak she managed to yell out, 'QUINN, IT'S ME!'

She saw his eyes light up and his grin widen. He turned in her direction and she prepared to shout out a second time, only to be overwhelmed by an explosive roar behind her as another person shouted out, 'QUINN, IT'S ME!' The crowd must have thought this was some slogan as it spread quickly, until almost everyone was shouting out, 'QUINN,

IT'S ME!' Bethany was completely drowned out. She could see Quinn surveying the people waving at him, but Bethany was shoved and jostled by over-eager adults rushing to the barriers for a closer look.

The shouting reached fever pitch as the door of the limousine swung open and Quinn stepped out on to the tarmac. It was bizarre for Bethany to see him in a purely human form. His build was that of an extremely fat man, but with tapering arms and legs and an abnormally large head. No one else seemed to notice how odd this was, presumably thinking that it was some sort of costume.

Quinn gurgled with laughter. He took a few steps forward and stretched his arms out to silence the catcalls and shrieks of, 'QUINN, IT'S ME!' The crowd fell silent and looked at him in awe. He laughed a second time, a hoarse, throaty, spluttering sound. He pointed into the nearest section of the crowd. People looked at one another, then at Quinn, who motioned for them to move out of the way. One by one, the tight huddle separated, until Bethany found herself standing alone, Quinn pointing at her and nodding.

She was overcome with emotion. Her relief and elation at finally meeting him again was mixed with embarrassment at being the focal point for so many adults.

Quinn beckoned her forward and she strode over to the metal barrier where he stood. She felt self-conscious, knowing she had to maintain the act that she was just another fan and that she hadn't met Quinn before. The tingling sensation from her finger intensified and, glancing sideways, she saw a blur of black fur as the cat scampered out of the crowd.

'Quinn,' she said breathlessly, aware that loads of people were scrutinising her.

He tittered uncontrollably. He removed a small pink and yellow box from his pocket and leaned forward to present it to Bethany.

She reached out for it and whispered under her breath, 'We don't have much time. The leprechauns are after you. You need to tell me what is going on.' In a louder voice she said, 'Thank you for my gift. I feel honoured.'

The crowd applauded.

Quickly, in the burst of noise, she asked, 'Is it something to do with the demon?'

Quinn tittered, nodding his head. Up close, he looked even stranger. It was almost as if the human form was struggling to contain him. His face seemed to shimmer uncertainly. His eyes, in particular, wavered with flickering light.

'It *is* to do with the demon?' Bethany whispered again, unsure if he was confirming her question or acknowledging his fans.

He winked and tapped the box he had given her, then stepped back and raised his arms once more. It must have been a signal to his staff as they hurried into position, each standing by pink and yellow boxes as large as dustbins. They pressed important red buttons on the front of the boxes and fireworks burst from the openings. Several glittering streams arced through the air and exploded in impressive sprays above the crowd. Rockets whizzed and whirled, colours popped and crackled. And even though it was daytime, the display turned the sky a series of dazzling pinks and vivid yellows. Everyone gasped and oohed and aahed with wonder. Bethany barely noticed. She shouted at Quinn as she saw the black cat weaving in and out of the fence and stopping a few feet from her. It hissed.

'Quinn. The cat!'

He swivelled his head, giggled uncontrollably, and aimed his finger at the black cat. A blue crackle of energy burst from his finger. In response, the cat arched its back and sent out its own surge of energy. A burst of orange light repelled Quinn's magic, causing jagged sparks to rebound off the ground and fence, crackling as loudly as one of the fireworks. The bystanders shrieked, thinking that this was part of the show. Luckily, the sparks missed the surrounding group, but Bethany felt something burning strike her hand and she dropped the box Quinn had given her.

As the fireworks display ended, an enlarged image of Quinn's face filled the sky, made up of hundreds of pinpoints of light. There was unanimous cheering. Quinn redoubled his attacks on the cat but it managed to deflect the bolts of energy with its own magic and the resulting blast tore a hole in the metal barrier. The group behind it screeched at the explosion, then examined the hole. A few of them rushed towards Quinn as if drawn to him. 'QUINN, IT'S ME!' they shouted giddily.

Bethany caught sight of the box on the ground and managed to scoop it up before it was trampled underfoot by adults keen to get through the broken barrier. The cat scampered off and Quinn retreated to his limousine as several fans neared him. Cameras flashed, people cheered, the car accelerated off in a squeal of spinning tyres.

'There you are,' she heard her father say to her.

Bethany turned round and saw her parents approaching. 'Sorry, I wanted to get to the front,' she explained.

Mr Chase gave a small frown. 'I know, we saw. Please don't run off like that again. If this crowd had been any bigger we could have lost sight of you.'

She nodded her head.

'Never mind that,' Mrs Chase said, clapping her hands with uncontained glee. 'You were picked out. So what was it? What did he give you? Anything good?'

She sounded so breathless and excited that Bethany and her father both turned to her for a moment.

'What? It's exciting. You met Quinn,' Mrs Chase said defensively.

Bethany examined the pink and yellow box in her hand. She felt apprehensive about opening it in front of her parents. After all, whatever it was, Quinn had meant it for her alone and it could be difficult to explain why he knew her.

'Open it. Open it,' her mother said quickly.

'Well . . .' Bethany replied, unsure. She checked around her for any signs of the cat, fearful that it might be ready to attack her now that Quinn had left. Carefully, she slipped the lid off the box, opening it as if it might explode. She peeked inside before her parents could see, checking there was nothing incriminating.

'Come on,' Mrs Chase squealed. 'What is it?'

'That's weird,' Bethany said, showing them the inside of the box. 'It's completely empty.'

CHAPTER EIGHT

SUMMONED

'I must say, you always have such interesting days out,' Aunt Bess remarked as she laid out one of her homemade sponges. 'Anyone for cake?'

Bethany and her parents eyed the cake, then the cats slinking around the kitchen worktops. They all politely declined.

Mrs Chase eagerly laid out the contents of their goodie bag on to the table. There was a mixture of Quinn merchandise: a bottle of aftershave, Quinn brand toothpaste, several packets of Facetoffees and Fizzbombs, Quinn brand moisturising lotion, and a packet of hair dye. Mrs Chase was sorting the various packets and boxes into piles. 'I've given you the sweets, Bethany,' she told her daughter. 'I think it's only fair that I take the hair dye.'

Mrs Chase's immaculate hair had faded somewhat since the previous day and looked strangely drab and lifeless.

'I'm fine, thanks. You can keep the sweets if you like,' Bethany replied. She couldn't help noticing that Aunt Bess seemed quiet. 'I think I would prefer a bit of cake after all,' she said, helping herself to a slice of the jammy sponge.

This cheered her aunt up immediately and Bethany made a great show of enjoying it, even though it wasn't long before she picked out a tortoiseshell cat hair from the sponge. 'It's very nice,' she lied.

'Do you think so?' Aunt Bess beamed. 'I was nearly going to stop with the baking. I wasn't sure I had the knack but . . . you know, I think you've given me the confidence to keep going. Thank you, Bethany.'

Mr Chase rolled his eyes. Idly, he examined the bottle of aftershave, dabbing some on to his fingers. It had a strong and clear scent of pine forests, so clear that Bethany was sure she could detect the smell of sap and of fresh mountain air among the odour of the trees.

As her mother babbled on to Aunt Bess about the firework display, Bethany thought about the box, Quinn and the cat. *What had he been trying to give her? Or had it been another one of his pranks?* No, she was sure that the box contained something important that must have been knocked out of it during the struggle. She just couldn't figure out what it was. She was furious with the cat for ruining her one chance to get some answers from Quinn, but she was also furious with herself for not pursuing him more forcefully when she had the chance. She wanted to warn him of the danger he was in.

The rest of the day dragged and Bethany moped in her cramped bedroom. She turned the box over in her hand again and again before dumping it into a pile of nearby suitcases. She stared through her window, fully expecting to see the black cat gloating at her, but noticed nothing unusual. She wished Quinn had been able to explain to her more about what was going on. He seemed to have confirmed that the demon was involved somehow but she didn't know in what way. Her thoughts leaped to the Jackomuss demon and its malignant nature. *Has it come back?* she thought to herself. *Is that what's after me?*

It gave her a chill just thinking about it, and Bethany was glad when it was time to go to bed. She had almost forgotten about the leprechauns and their strange world. She thought she was dreaming their voices as she began to stir from the edge of sleep.

'Just try and protect her against the curses,' Flannigan was saying. 'We'll be as quick as we can.'

'But I thought you said we were going to take it in turns,' Donovan complained.

'Ah, sure I did now,' Flannigan admitted. 'But you know I'm not to be trusted, Donovan. Now get in the pot.'

Bethany managed to get out of bed and was running desperately for the door when she saw the flash of gold. There was a forceful shove as she was expelled from her body and she fell back on to the mattress in her spirit form, disorientated. Pat sprinkled a handful of his glittering powder over her, reciting '*yeartha don toory.*' Her spirit body shrank in response and she soon found herself the same size as the leprechauns.

'You don't seem to be happy to see us,' Seamus noted with a grin.

Bethany shot him a dark look. 'Why would I? I don't remember last time being a particularly nice day out.'

'Quick, quick,' Flannigan said urgently. He thrust Bethany towards the window ledge, where the Mineral Underground was waiting for them.

'I told you, I don't want anything to do with you, Flannigan. You're just going to get me in to more trouble,' she snapped at him in an angry tone.

'You know, you're right there,' he agreed as the doors closed behind them. 'But I don't make the rules.'

There was the *ding-ding* sound of the bell and the train pulled off, curling into a downwards spiral. Bethany grabbed the nearest cluster of diamonds and held on as tightly as she could. The train executed a series of impossibly sharp and sudden manoeuvres.

'You're being summoned,' Seamus explained as he leaned over and tapped the ring on Bethany's finger. She could see it clearly now that she was in the spirit realm, the green jewel had started glinting regularly like a flashing light.

'It's been making my hand tingle,' she said.

'It is sensitive to curses,' Flannigan said in a quiet voice.

'Although I'm sure you wouldn't have noticed anything like that as you would have stayed at home and not done anything remotely dangerous or risky. Like I told you.'

'Um, yeah . . . no, of course,' she corrected herself. She had wanted to tell them about Quinn but wondered whether Flannigan would be displeased with her. *Not now,* she thought. *Maybe I'll tell him later, otherwise it'll just cause problems. And anyway, there's plenty they don't tell me.* She glanced over at Pat. He was making a strange face at Bethany, frowning then jerking his head to one side. It didn't look particularly comfortable. 'Are you OK, Pat?' she asked.

'Fine,' he muttered. 'It's just a busy train today.'

Bethany wasn't entirely sure what he meant by this until she looked around the carriage and noticed the slumped, lumpy form of Hurm Igrig sitting several seats away from them. He was busily studying a bundle of papers with a grave expression, his bushy eyebrows caught in such a heavy frown that it was amazing he could read anything at all.

'What's *he* doing here?' Bethany whispered angrily. She didn't like Hurm Igrig. There was something extremely distrustful about him that she couldn't quite explain, as if he was toying with her in some way.

'Not sure,' the leprechaun replied cautiously. 'Might be that he's keeping an eye on us before the trial.'

'What?'

'You know, to check we're not planning any surprises.'

Bethany didn't follow. She was under the impression that

she was giving evidence. 'Why would we be preparing surprises? I'm just a witness, aren't I?'

The three leprechauns shifted in their seats awkwardly.

Flannigan tried to sound chatty and informal. 'Well, now, the thing is, you're not the witness. You're the other one. You know, the, um . . . what's it called?'

'The accused,' Pat said.

'The WHAT?' Bethany screeched. The entire carriage looked up. Several leprechauns at the far end were so startled that they let go of their diamonds and fell sideways. Hurm Igrig pretended not to notice, casually flipping through his papers, but Bethany could see a smirk curling his lips. 'And you . . . !' she called out threateningly, almost taking a step out of her seat.

Flannigan pulled her back into her chair and hissed in her ear. 'Calm down. What do you think you're doing, girl?'

Bethany fumed. Her spirit body glowed red like a burning ember. It took her a few moments to compose herself before she said in a careful whisper, 'Explain what's going on, Flannigan.'

'You are standing trial as Quinn's accomplice. That meeting you had with Hurm Igrig decided it. You told him you would help Quinn. It was enough for him to start court proceedings against you.'

'But all I said was that I would help him if he was in trouble,' Bethany protested. 'I thought Quinn was on trial and I was going to be a witness. I mean, I've not *done anything*, Flannigan.'

He could see she was getting agitated and tried to reassure her. 'I know. I'm sure it will be fine,' he whispered back at her. 'The thing is, you're being made a scapegoat. News of the stolen gold has spread and someone has to be seen to be punished. It's impossible to get near to Quinn in the physical realm – he's far too powerful with all that gold – so they've decided to target you. It'll reassure the general leprechaun population if they can see that someone is standing trial over it. But everything will be OK. As long as you've not had any contact with him, we'll sail through the court case.'

'Oh,' Bethany said in a quiet voice. She thought to herself, *Well, that's that! I'm going to have to tell him now.* The train descended into the ground, accelerating through the dark subterranean layers below London, and Bethany felt her mood drop with it. She chewed her lip and tried to think of some reasonable way to put it. 'Um . . . look, I . . . well, the thing is . . .' She uttered a low humming noise then blurted it out, 'I saw Quinn. I'm sorry, I know you said not to, but I had to at least try. He helped me in the spirit hotel when things were bad and I wanted to repay the favour.'

'You WHAT?' Flannigan screeched. The passengers in the carriage looked up a second time at this outburst. Bethany was sure she could hear the *hmmff hmmff hmmff* of Hurm Igrig discreetly chortling to himself. She glowered at him before returning her attention to Flannigan. The leprechaun, realising how loud he had been, lowered his voice to the thinnest of whispers. 'I told you to do nothing.

I told you to stay away from him. Have you any idea how much trouble you have put yourself in? How am I supposed to defend you if you behave like this?'

'But I . . . *you're* going to defend me in court?' Bethany replied incredulously.

'Of course,' Flannigan snapped. 'For all the good it will do me.'

Pat and Seamus confirmed this with proud expressions. 'He's got a wig and everything,' Seamus told Bethany, as if this would answer any concerns she might have.

'Then don't you want to know what happened when I saw him?' Bethany asked.

Flannigan's face became stern. He folded his arms. 'Absolutely not.'

'But —'

The leprechaun rounded on her. 'It's incredibly risky for you at the moment. You should not be making contact with him. He's a wanted criminal. He's responsible for the biggest theft of leprechaun gold in our history.'

Bethany interrupted him, moving closer and dropping her voice. 'But what if he stole it for a reason?' She looked down the carriage to check Hurm Igrig wasn't eavesdropping and spoke quietly and urgently. 'I think he might be after a demon. Seamus said that Quinn had become a demon hunter, and I think he has chased a demon into the physical realm. It appears as the black cat, but it doesn't act like a cat. It casts spells and it has a lot of power.'

Flannigan looked uncertain. He scratched his beard.

Bethany persisted. 'I've been thinking, what if Quinn was after the Jackomuss demon? I saw it escape, Flannigan. What if Quinn tracked it down? What if he needed strong magic to fight it in the physical realm?'

'It's not going to help you thinking like this,' he replied quickly, but she could see that the idea had stumped him. He wore a look of intense concentration.

Bethany was still not sure what Quinn was doing. There was a piece missing from the jigsaw, but she knew that he was innocent. He played tricks and caused no end of mischief, but he was not evil as the leprechauns believed.

'You might be on to something,' Flannigan conceded eventually. 'But I quizzed Donovan about the black cat, and he didn't see it once when he was in your body. It could be that if there is a demon, it might have the power to track your spirit. Still, I'm not sure if —'

Seamus nudged him. He murmured without moving his lips, 'He's looking over. Act normal.'

The three leprechauns and Bethany stopped talking and tried to appear as normal as they could. Cautiously, Bethany glanced at Hurm Igrig and noticed that his attention was lingering on them. His immense nose twitched and sniffed at the air as if he was trying to detect a smell. After a long pause, he dismissed the concerns and returned to his papers.

'No more talk on the train,' Flannigan muttered. 'Too risky. He'll sniff us out.'

They remained in silence for the rest of the journey. This allowed Bethany to overhear snippets of conversation from the other spirits in the carriage. From what she could tell, the trial was the main topic among the leprechauns. Eyes glared at her furtively, then turned away. Bethany was sure she could hear her own name, although not in admiring tones but in suspicious gossipy mutterings.

As the Mineral Underground pulled into the station, they could see a crowd waiting for them on the platform. There were leprechauns in official blue uniforms holding back a mob of bustling spirits. There were groups in red hats with sneering, angry expressions, suspicious huddles in brown hats, and clusters of curious leprechauns in white hats stretching their necks to get a glimpse of Bethany.

'Ah, would you look at that now?' Flannigan groaned. 'Bad news travels fast.'

'Someone must have told them,' Pat added, glancing at Hurm Igrig.

Bethany felt naive and foolish for not realising the importance of the trial. 'Oh, this is a big deal, isn't it?' she sighed despairingly, looking at all the faces turning towards her.

Seamus nearly spluttered with laughter. 'Big deal, girl? There's never been a trial like it. And you, a human, once a hero. Well, it doesn't get bigger than this.'

Her heart sank. '*Once* a hero?'

'Just stay by my side,' Flannigan instructed her as they made it to the doorway. She barely had time to answer before the train stopped and the doors opened. Bethany was thrust on to the platform and dragged forwards by

Flannigan, staying close to him as he ploughed through the gauntlet of yelling and jeering leprechauns. The air above them flashed with colour as some of them threw up handfuls of their magical dust. Bethany could briefly see a three-dimensional image of herself caught in the specks of dust, as if she was having her photo taken.

Flannigan pulled her on. Angry faces snarled at her from the crowd, while others inspected her as if she was some sort of unusual animal on parade. She even saw several groups cheering for her and waving banners of light emblazoned with her face. This was too much. She wanted to run back to the train and escape, but found it was impossible to even turn round.

Pat lunged forward as several objects were thrown from the clamouring edge of the mob. He knocked the objects out of the air and Bethany saw one land at her feet. It was a miniature statue of Quinn and herself, much like the one she had seen on her previous visit, although it had the word *THIEVES* scrawled across it. Another three were pelted at her, and she shouted back at the crowd in protest, 'I didn't do anything!'

Seamus and Flannigan hurried her up a short set of steps and on to a waiting chair. This one had two rows of seats and a ghost driver. The chair appeared to have the lower body of a large lizard and was, mercifully for Bethany, extremely near to the ground. She was wedged into the back seat with Pat and Seamus on each side. Flannigan sat in the row in front and motioned for the ghost to move forward.

The lizard legs sprang into action. Briefly, Bethany peered back and saw Hurm Igrig in his black suit, calmly poised on the top of a tortoise-legged chair, looking decidedly smug as he set off after them.

She opened her mouth to speak, brimming with anger and confusion and shock from her exposure to the mob, but she burst into tears. The sobs racked her body and the leprechauns nervously reassured her, patting her shoulder. 'They hate me,' she cried. 'I haven't even done anything. I don't want to be here. It's not my fault, Flannigan. It's not my fault.'

'Come on, girl. It's not all that bad,' Flannigan said.

Bethany tried to quell the stream of tears, sniffing and spluttering. 'It's not?'

'I mean, sure, you're accused of being an accomplice to one of the biggest crimes in leprechaun history.'

'And you're up against Hurm Igrig, one of the toughest prosecutors that has ever graced a court,' Seamus mentioned idly.

'And you've got the weight of public opinion against you,' Pat added.

Bethany managed to stop crying to peer at the leprechauns. '*But?*' she asked hopefully.

Pat, Seamus and Flannigan looked at her blankly for a moment. 'Oh, um . . . but at least you've got us,' Flannigan announced brightly.

She let out a huge wailing sob and dropped her head into her hands. The leprechauns exchanged worried glances.

114

Flannigan swung round in his seat, causing Pat and Seamus to lean forward so that they formed a tight huddle. The leprechauns muttered to one another. Between her sobs, Bethany caught snippets of conversation: '. . . Need to let her know . . . still be strong enough . . . but this trial . . . too late now . . . stick to the plan!'

The lizard chair made quick work of the busy roads leading to the centre of the Stolen City. The ghost chauffeur guided them through packed lines of travelling leprechauns, dodging and winding past the other chairs. Bethany heard her name called several times and tried to ignore it. She pulled herself together. 'What are we going to do?' she asked Flannigan.

He fixed her with a sincere expression. 'Don't worry. I'll take care of the trial. Seamus will see if he can find out anything about the cat or about the demons Quinn was hunting. Just keep your cool in the court.'

Ahead of them, the justice building rose into view. The clockwork construction towered above them as they approached the wide stairways leading to the entrance. There was something off-putting about the mass of cogs and wheels moving in precise motions, something inevitable and ominous.

'You'd better know what you're doing,' Bethany warned him. 'None of this would have happened if you hadn't exaggerated so much about what we did in the spirit hotel. I wouldn't be a hero here. I wouldn't be known as a friend of Quinn's. I would just be a normal nobody.'

Flannigan held up his hands in apology. 'And there was

me thinking I was doing you a favour. Isn't it funny how things work out?'

'No,' Bethany replied flatly, jabbing a finger at him in a threatening manner. 'No, it's not funny.'

The leprechauns flinched at her sudden fury and all dismounted the chair as quickly as they could. Crowds were gathering at the edges of the steps, but were kept at a safe distance by a transparent barrier that sparkled with light whenever a waiting spirit pressed against it. Bethany hurried up the steps, ignoring the shouts and jeers, and was surprised to see that Hurm Igrig had already made it to the entrance and was casually chatting to a colleague as if he had been waiting there most of the day. She checked over her shoulder. The tortoise chair was standing obediently at the bottom of the stairs.

'How did he do that?' she wondered aloud.

Pat mumbled in her ear, incoherently at first, then more clearly. 'All sorts of magic, that one. Very powerful leprechaun, he is. High up and all of that, which means he can do almost anything he likes. If you take my advice you'll watch out for him.'

Pat fell silent as they passed directly by Hurm Igrig. The older leprechaun acknowledged them all with a nod of his head and a wide, polite grin. 'Frannigan. Bethany Chase. I wish you the best of luck today and look forward to hearing your robust defence.'

Out of habit, Flannigan nodded meekly. 'Yes . . . well, um, thank you, sir.'

Bethany nudged him in the ribs and hissed in his ear. 'Be more bold.'

Flannigan pulled himself upright and tried his best to sound confident. 'It's Flannigan, sir. And my client and I are in a hurry. We will see you in court.'

Hurm Igrig's bushy eyebrows twitched in surprise (and maybe, thought Bethany, partly in admiration). 'Well, let us at least hope for a speedy resolution to the case.'

As if on cue, a bell let out a series of chimes. Flannigan consulted the jewelled ring on his finger, which was glowing with a ghostly white flame. The gemstone on Bethany's ring had similarly changed from flashing green to this more urgent flickering state. The groups of official-looking leprechauns filed into the entranceway.

'It's time,' Flannigan announced flatly. He faced Pat and Seamus. 'You better get busy. We'll see you after the verdict.'

The two leprechauns nodded.

'Don't worry, girl,' Seamus said with a wink. 'You'll be fine.'

Pat gave her a sly, secretive smile as if he was trying to hold in a laugh. 'What could go wrong?' he chuckled.

They both walked off before Bethany could reply. Flannigan was marching her away in the opposite direction. He seemed impatient, as if nerves were getting the better of him, and that made Bethany even more worried about what they were facing. He weaved through the busy lobby and into a spacious hall. Numerous doors confronted them as they faced a tall curved section of wall that was turning at regular intervals like a huge cylindrical piece of clockwork. With each loud TICK and TOCK, the doors advanced one place, and leprechauns of all types were scampering through the shifting entrances. Flannigan hesitated as he read the two sets of signs. One set was written on the door and moved with the rotating wall. The other set was written on a separate section above the doorways and was fixed in one place.

BEFORE	NOW	LATER	MUCH LATER
COURT OF	COURT OF	COURT OF	COURT OF
MAJOR CRIMES	MINOR CRIMES	SENTENCING	APPEALS

Bethany watched as the line of doors shifted forward one space with the next TICK.

BEFORE	NOW	LATER	MUCH LATER
COURT OF	COURT OF	COURT OF	COURT OF
INVESTIGATIONS	MAJOR CRIMES	MINOR CRIMES	SENTENCING

'Well, this makes things nice and simple,' Bethany commented sarcastically. 'Which one do we go through?'

Flannigan scratched his chin. 'We need the Court of Major Crimes. I need to be there now, but you don't need to be there until much later.'

She groaned at him. 'What do you mean later? Shouldn't I be there with you now?'

'No, no,' he said emphatically. 'The less you know about the court case, the better. It will make you appear more innocent to the jury.' He looked up and saw the door he needed passing underneath the NOW sign. 'I have to go. Don't be early.'

With a carefully timed leap, Flannigan disappeared through the entrance, leaving Bethany on her own. She had to wait for the door to complete a circuit to synchronise with the MUCH LATER sign. It felt strange being suddenly alone after all the crowds of leprechauns and she had to fight the impulse to run away. She was certain that if she tried to escape she would be caught before she even made it to the Mineral Underground.

As the door slid round, the ring on her finger guided her forward, gently tugging her finger and leading her through the correct door. She found herself on a set of rising stairs that, on closer inspection, was a huge turning cog lifting her up to a set of double doors. She could feel herself being passed through the vast, complex pieces of clockwork whirring and ticking around her, unable to stop it or influence it in any way.

You'll be fine, she thought to herself as she approached the double doors. *You'll be fine. You're completely innocent. They will be able to see that and it will all be fine. There's nothing to panic about.* She tried to summon up all her courage as she stepped through.

Bethany had never been inside a courtroom before, but had a vague idea of what sort of thing to expect. It came as somewhat of a shock, then, as she walked through the doors and found herself in a vast and packed auditorium facing hundreds of leprechauns gathered in row after row of seats.

The rows collected into balconies and the balconies stacked up on top of one another, so high that it made her dizzy looking up at the top line of seats. They were not sitting quietly or respectfully as she thought would have been customary in a court. Instead, they were cheering and talking and comparing magic with one another, conjuring ghostly images in the air around them. Some of those images, Bethany was sure, contained glimpses of herself and Quinn. At her arrival their behaviour seemed to worsen, some applauding, some booing, some rising to their feet to hurl insults.

Nervously, Bethany shuffled forward.

CHAPTER NINE

CAUGHT IN COURT

'Order in court!' a voice boomed.

A mallet repeatedly banged against a wooden base. The voice and sounds of the mallet were greatly amplified through some charmed process and quelled the general clamour of the seated spirits. The auditorium gradually fell into a respectful silence. The judge sat in a tall, important box at the centre of the courtroom so that he could oversee proceedings. He was an elderly leprechaun, with an immensely long white beard and all sorts of jewellery covering his body. There were chunky rings on each finger, glittering bangles on his wrists and dazzling chains draped about his neck. Bethany could just about make out his disgruntled face beneath an elaborate wig that he had ingeniously formed out of the end of his trailing beard. 'The court calls Bethany Chase,' he announced.

A guard in a blue uniform appeared before Bethany and led her towards a raised platform. A chair sprouted from the ground to accommodate her, and she found herself sitting down, facing the packed auditorium. Directly in front of her were two desks. Hurm Igrig occupied the desk to her right, covering it in neat stacks of paper and a row of bejewelled rings like the ones she had seen in his office. He was wearing official black robes and a white wig, and he generated an air of importance and authority. In comparison, Flannigan was nattily dressed, his wig leaning at an angle, his tatty robes hanging limply from his shoulders. His desk was almost completely bare, with only a few scraps of scrunched-up paper surrounding him, covered with what looked suspiciously like doodles. She could guess by his appearance alone that the trial had not gone well up until now.

'Confirm your name for the court,' instructed the judge in a weary tone.

Bethany looked up at him, then surveyed the court and the auditorium. Nervously, she said, 'Bethany Chase.'

This caused an uproarious response from the audience of leprechauns. They howled with laughter.

'Silence!' the judge snapped testily. 'The jury are reminded that they are here to pass judgement on the defendant and should approach that task with the utmost respect and honour.'

The packed balconies tittered uneasily, before eventually falling back into hushed muttering.

That's the jury? Bethany thought incredulously. She stared at the hundreds upon hundreds of misbehaving spirits and was overcome with dread. This was worse than she thought.

'Please use the ring,' the judge said irritably.

Confused, she shot a desperate look at Flannigan and he pointed to the ring on her hand, miming for her to move it to the index finger of her left hand. She placed the band of gold on that finger and, almost shaking with nerves, spoke her name again. This time her voice was amplified so that it carried throughout the entire courtroom. 'Bethany Chase.'

The judge nodded with satisfaction, then waved at the guard, who moved forwards and placed a flickering object into Bethany's hands. She found herself holding a dancing white flame. It did not give off heat like a normal flame but filled her with a pleasant sensation, calming and energising.

'Repeat after me,' the guard said to Bethany. 'I, Bethany Chase, do hereby give my evidence to the Court of Lupre in defence of the pooka known as Quinn. I will bear all judgements placed upon me.'

Bethany looked to Flannigan again for help and he urged her on. She repeated the statement word for word, trying not to sound uncertain or nervous or dwell too much on what 'judgements' might involve. It was unnerving hearing her own voice carried so loudly, but the leprechauns, Flannigan, Hurm Igrig and the judge all wore blank expressions, as if this was an entirely familiar procedure. The guard retrieved the white flame from her hands.

'Prosecution,' the judge sighed, gesturing for Hurm Igrig to rise to his feet.

'Your honour.' He gave a respectful bow to the judge. He spun on his heels. 'Noble jurors.' The rabble of the auditorium made pleasing, flattered sounds. 'The defence.' He stated this in a disdainful, pitying tone that provoked sniggering from large sections of the jury.

Hurm Igrig strode to the centre of the court. His gestures had become exaggerated. His body language had become bold and theatrical. He held his arms out to the platform where Bethany was seated as if presenting a star attraction. 'And Bethany Chase, slayer of demons, honoured hero of the leprechauns and . . . *the accused*.'

His voice rang out. There was a mixed response of applause and boos directed at Bethany. Hurm Igrig's knobbly face stretched into a gesture of mock surprise. He held up both hands to the chorus of jeering. 'Please, jurors, I beseech you . . . do not judge this girl before she has had a chance to speak. Yes, maybe the evidence you have seen so far is overwhelming. Maybe it has been proven beyond reasonable doubt that Quinn has committed the most heinous act of theft known to us. And maybe you think that the human spirit you see before you, the closest ally Quinn has, has been an accomplice to that crime, but please . . . keep an open mind until she has spoken.'

Hurm Igrig paced back towards his desk, having expertly commanded the attention of everyone in the courtroom.

Bethany could hardly believe the transformation that had come over him, the way his sagging face had become so animated, capable of expressing kindness, indignation and sincerity so expertly and with such speed. She exchanged a furtive glance with Flannigan and noticed how small and defeated her friend looked.

'What evidence?' Bethany blurted out.

Hurm Igrig stopped in his tracks and stared at her in surprise. The judge peered down from his raised box, unsure of what he had just heard. Shocked whispers passed between the rows of leprechauns.

'What evidence are you talking about?' she said more confidently. By the reaction she was getting, it was not customary to ask questions in a direct manner like this. She didn't care. 'I've not had the chance to hear the evidence. I'm the one who's on trial here.'

Hurm Igrig's dark bushy eyebrows collected in a flummoxed frown. 'Well,' he said, clearly shocked at her outspokenness. He harrumphed.

Flannigan sank into his chair, wearing a horrified expression.

'Let me see if I can refresh the case for you.' Hurm Igrig picked a jewelled ring from the line of rings on his desk. There was a similar projecting rod like the one he had used in his office and he fixed the ring into place. This device must have been much stronger than the previous one Bethany had seen, though, as it cast a gigantic sphere of light that filled most of the immediate courtroom.

The image was cast by the ring of a female leprechaun wearing a white uniform who appeared to be in the leprechaun equivalent of a bank. The leprechaun and numerous guards were all tied up and gagged, watching helplessly as Quinn raided the contents of a vault stacked with pots of gold. He had found the biggest pots and was filling them to the brim with the mysterious golden substance, then stacking as many as he could on a rug that he had charmed to float beside him. Once he had filled the rug with as many pots as it could carry he made his getaway, and, as if to gloat over his misdeeds, he stopped and grinned at his captors before he left.

'Quinn stealing the gold,' Hurm Igrig stated plainly. He quickly replaced the ring with another.

The next scene projected above them showed a street in the city. Bethany briefly recognised some of the buildings in the background, including the justice building. This ring appeared to belong to a street seller of some sort. The leprechaun, in bright orange garments, was selling cups of cloud tea to passing pedestrians from a decorative cart. He was standing in front of a grandiose domed building with statues of what were presumably important leprechauns mounted on its balconies. The street seller looked up as the statues, one by one, began to move, their jaws dropping open and issuing a chorus of shrieks, like the sound of a rising alarm bell. The reason for this became apparent as Quinn burst out of the doors, with his floating rug laden with piles of glowing pots. He ran past the street vendor, again stopping near to the ring so that his face was clearly visible as he gurgled with laughter. He moved the rug to a waiting chair – a large elephant-legged chair that was already rising in motion as he approached. A pair of strange ghostly figures were guiding the chair for Quinn, shrunken down in size to match the leprechauns. Bethany could hardly believe her eyes as the recording showed a pair of elderly conjoined twins, the ghost sisters that Bethany had last seen as cleaning ladies in the spirit hotel.

'Maggie-Maggie,' she called out without thinking.

Hurm Igrig's bulbous nose twitched and quivered, and he could barely contain a satisfied smirk. He paused the recording. 'If it pleases the court, the accused has identified the ghosts Maggie-Maggie.'

'Duly noted,' grumbled the judge.

Flannigan sank deeper into his chair and shook his head despairingly, and Bethany knew she had done something wrong.

Hurm Igrig pointed his finger at the projection, the edge of the image rippling like disrupted water. 'This was Quinn escaping with his other accomplice.'

'Accomplice? But that's Maggie-Maggie,' Bethany said in frustration. 'She's not bad.'

The elderly leprechaun purposefully let the comment linger, turning to the auditorium and making a face that seemed to encourage the widespread sighing and tutting of the crowd. 'The ghosts Maggie-Maggie have already been found guilty of aiding a known criminal.'

Bethany felt her face flush red with a mixture of frustration and embarrassment. She wanted to shout out, to make the jury see that Maggie-Maggie was innocent, just as Bethany was, but she felt hopeless and confused by the evidence of what she was watching. Whereas Quinn had a mischievous side, Bethany knew that the ghost sisters were incapable of the slightest act of malice. If they had been found guilty, what chance did Bethany have of a fair outcome? Flannigan did not help matters by holding up a sign that simply read, *STOP TALKING*.

'But . . .' Bethany felt flustered and overwhelmed.

Hurm Igrig continued, picking out the next ring. This played the footage Bethany had previously seen of the officer involved in trying to halt Quinn at the Mineral Underground, except it began from an earlier point this time. It showed the officer intercepting Quinn and Maggie-Maggie outside the station. A troop of the leprechaun officers became involved in the violent exchange of magic with the pooka. Bethany noticed how terrified Maggie-Maggie appeared as Quinn escaped into the station, leaving her behind. She looked confused and alarmed, certainly not like a willing accomplice should.

Hurm Igrig must have known, Bethany thought suddenly. In his office, he had shown her the footage *after* Maggie-Maggie, because he must have known Bethany would recognise the ghost sisters. He had let it come as a surprise now, to make her look more guilty. She was being manipulated.

The projected images finished playing. 'Well?' Hurm

Igrig said in a smug tone. He strode in front of Bethany.

She could hardly answer. She was feeling numb, unsure of how to react to his cunningness. *Why did he have it in for her?* 'Well, what?' she replied quietly.

'What do you make of the evidence so far?' he asked casually, as if he was making pleasant conversation.

She was sure it was a comment calculated to enrage her further. She had to make sure she didn't look stupid or fall into any more of his traps. Desperately, she tried to remain calm and block out the confused thoughts about Quinn, the cat and the leprechauns. She felt as if everyone was against her. 'I know how it looks,' she said carefully. 'But I know Quinn, and I know he wouldn't do something like this without a very good reason.'

Hurm Igrig nodded his head solemnly and returned to his desk to check his notes. 'You are closely associated with Quinn, are you not?'

Bethany pulled herself up in her seat. 'I know Quinn. Well, *knew* him.'

'And how did you know him?'

'We stopped a demon together. The demon was trapping spirits and ghosts in a hotel. It put people . . . spirits, *everything* into a trance, and it was feeding off them, making itself powerful. We stopped it.'

'You destroyed it?' Hurm Igrig asked.

'Well . . . sort of. It was a mixture of spirits joined together and controlled by the demon part. We destroyed it, but the demon part escaped.'

Hurm Igrig made a puzzled noise. 'But you and Quinn are known as demon *slayers*, are you not?'

'Yes, but that's not my fault. I mean, that's what you call me here in your city, but I never . . .' She struggled to find the right words. 'I've never called myself that.'

The leprechaun faced the auditorium, clutching the edges of his gown. 'But when I introduced you moments ago as Bethany Chase, slayer of demons, you did not correct me. And yet, if you are happy to be called a demon slayer when it suits you, it intrigues me that you have not slain the demon you are most famous for destroying. Tell me, are there any other demons you have killed?'

She felt her frustration growing. 'No, I haven't destroyed any other demons, but I never said I —'

'No other demons, honourable members of the jury,' Hurm Igrig said with a dramatic flourish, causing the mass of leprechauns to break into a disgruntled hubbub of noise as if Bethany had admitted a terrible secret.

'I never claimed to have killed any demons,' Bethany protested, but her voice was drowned out by the rising din. She peered out at the jury and saw hundreds of angry, disapproving faces. She felt furious with Flannigan. It was *his* fault for exaggerating what had happened.

'Order!' the judge called. He slammed his wooden mallet down several times. He seemed, for the most part, to be bored by the trial and was examining a band of sapphires encrusted on one of the golden chains around his neck.

When the crowd had calmed down Hurm Igrig

continued. 'Tell me, Bethany Chase, when did you last see Quinn?'

'I . . .' She tried to sound as steady as possible, even though her voice was becoming croaky with nerves. She decided that the only option was to tell the truth. That way there might be a vague possibility that the jury would realise she was not a liar. 'I saw him yesterday.'

There was a whoosh of noise as the jury gasped. It was followed by a wave of muttering, outraged and scornful.

Hurm Igrig clasped his hands behind his back and collected his bushy eyebrows into a tight frown of concentration. 'You met him in the physical realm?'

'Yes, but I . . . I mean, no. I didn't *meet* him exactly. That makes it sound as though we arranged it. I saw him with lots of other people. It was a public appearance.' Bethany was feeling that she was incriminating herself no matter what she said. Flannigan would not even meet her gaze. She was furious with him for being so useless, and wanted to run over and shake him by the shoulders to shock him into action. A tense silence settled over the court as if the trial had become a serious matter for the jury.

The leprechaun used the moment to perfect effect. 'I ask you, Bethany Chase, are you in collusion with Quinn the pooka?'

'No! No, I'm not.'

'Have you been making contact with him so that you can take your share of the gold?'

The anger and frustration rose in her. 'No. That's

ridiculous,' she shouted. 'How could I have been involved in stealing the gold when I didn't even know it existed until a few weeks ago? I didn't even know this city existed.'

'And yet your statue graces our streets,' Hurm Igrig scoffed. He made a low exasperated sound. 'Do you expect us to believe that?'

'It's true!' Bethany protested. Her spirit body flushed a deep scarlet colour.

'Next you will be telling us that it is just a coincidence that you are in the same city in the physical realm as Quinn, at the same time, meeting by accident.' The tone was unmistakeably mocking and Bethany couldn't help herself. *All of this was so unfair.*

'IT'S NOT LIKE THAT!' she screeched. 'You're twisting everything I say.'

There was a stunned response to the force of her outburst. Even the judge leaned over to examine her. Startled, he muttered under his breath, 'Quite irregular.'

Hurm Igrig let the moment linger. In a very calm, cool voice that contrasted sharply with Bethany's impulsive screech, he spoke. 'Maybe you are right,' he conceded (although in such a way that she felt he was patronising her). 'Maybe I am twisting your words.' He took several steps towards her and held out his hand. His lumpy, sagging face surveyed her dolefully, and for the briefest moment there was a glint of colour from beneath his eyebrows like a spark of fire. 'Ring, please,' he requested.

This threw Bethany for a moment. Something shifted

uncomfortably at the back of her mind. An uneasy thought momentarily distracted her. Clumsily, she removed the ring from her finger and passed it over to him. She felt her hands shaking.

'Thank you.' There was a tone to this that Bethany couldn't quite place – not exactly smugness, but something self-assured. The leprechaun took the ring and placed it on the end of the projecting rod so that a huge sphere projected above them with Bethany at the centre of it. She tried to ignore the embarrassment at seeing herself on such a large scale. Hurm Igrig altered some element of the rod so that the images sped backwards like a rewinding film. He quickly found what he was looking for. And Bethany's heart sank with realisation at what he was doing.

'For the benefit of the court, can you confirm this is a recording of you?' he asked.

She gritted her teeth and reluctantly nodded her head. She knew what he was going to show and knew what reaction it would get.

Hurm Igrig played the footage.

The ring had recorded all her experiences, including her meeting with Quinn at the supermarket the day before. These pictures were of a different quality to the ones in the spirit realm. There was the solid aspect of the real world, but with strange smears and glowing patterns of the spirit realm superimposed over it. Bethany cringed. *No, not this.* She knew it was all innocent, but that didn't matter. Any meeting with Quinn would look bad. She could barely watch as she saw the recording of herself.

She looked up at the image of her moving towards the metal barriers to make it closer to Quinn as he arrived in his stretch limousine. At the first sign of the pooka emerging from the car the auditorium exploded in angry shouts and catcalls. In the footage, Bethany was picked from the crowd by Quinn. She heard her own voice warning about the leprechauns, and the atmosphere in the court turned from anger to outright hostility. The most damning blow came as the images showed Bethany accepting the small box from Quinn. The box, far from looking empty as she had remembered it, seemed to contain a small glowing object. Whatever it was, it had a strong presence in the spirit realm, a presence that could easily be generated by a piece of leprechaun gold.

Bethany tried to explain, but without her ring to amplify her voice, no one could hear her. The balconies full of leprechauns began shouting angrily. Amid the cacophony of voices a chant started up. 'LIAR! LIAR! LIAR!' Rows of spirits stamped their feet in unison. As the rumbling, thundering din increased in fervency, several particularly enraged leprechauns jumped out of their seats and hurled crackling balls of magic towards Bethany.

She ducked as the guards rushed forward to protect her. She felt too shocked to know how to react.

'ORDER!' the judge called, rapping his mallet. He assumed a standing position and cast a spell across the auditorium. 'Tiny mouths!' he commanded, sending a flash of white light from his outstretched hand. The uproar instantly stopped as the entire mob of leprechauns had their mouths shrunken to a fraction of their normal size. The shouting sounded very distant and weak, and it was enough of a shock to force the jurors to fall back into their seats. They examined each other nervously, appalled by their tiny mouths, and stared humbly at the judge. Satisfied, he returned to his chair. 'That's better,' he remarked.

Bethany felt her face sting as if she was about to burst into tears. As Hurm Igrig appeared before her she forced her features into a stony expression, refusing to show any weakness in front of him. He passed the ring back to her. 'No hard feelings,' he told her. There was another glint from beneath his bushy eyebrows.

The judge raised his voice. 'Now then, has the prosecution any more questions for the accused?'

Hurm Igrig shook his head. 'No more questions, your honour.'

'Defence?'

Flannigan stirred and stood up. 'No questions, your honour,' he said. He took his seat again.

The judge peered down at Flannigan. 'Defence, did you hear me correctly?' he asked in a gruff tone. 'Or, more to the point, did I hear you correctly?'

'I did at that, your honour, and so did you. I have no questions.'

Hurm Igrig inspected his colleague with frank

amazement. Even the jury, having recovered from their shrunken mouths, gaped at Flannigan and muttered among themselves.

'But you're the defence. You are here to defend your client,' the judge reminded him. 'Are you sure you have no questions?'

'Well, if it's all the same to you, there's been an awful lot of questions already, so I won't bother.' He made it sound as if he was turning down the offer of a nice cup of tea.

Bethany was staring at Flannigan, unable to believe what she was hearing. *He was giving up without a fight. He wasn't even going to attempt to defend her.*

'Very well,' the judge sighed, and was about to hit his mallet to signify an end to the proceedings when Bethany leaped to her feet.

'What are you doing?!' she shouted at Flannigan. 'I thought you were going to help me! You're supposed to be my friend. How is *this* helping? Tell them what I told you about the cat. Tell them that Quinn might be after the Jackomuss demon. Tell them I'm innocent!'

Flannigan looked startled. 'I . . . erm . . . ah . . .'

Bethany turned to the judge. 'I've been followed by a cat in the physical realm. It has magical powers. I think it might be a demon of some sort. I think it is the demon we tried to destroy together and Quinn has been protecting me from it. I can't be certain but . . . he may have stolen that gold to make himself strong enough to fight it. Please, just play the rest of that recording. You'll see it. I'm not lying.'

Speechless, the judge eyed Bethany, then Flannigan, then Hurm Igrig, all with complete incomprehension. He finally managed to say, 'Very irregular.'

Hurm Igrig interrupted. 'Maybe I can shed some light on this.' He took the ring back off Bethany and placed it on to the projecting stand, returning it to the footage of Bethany meeting Quinn, although now he let it play. The cat appeared by the metal barriers. Like Quinn, it had a strong spirit that shimmered with light, and the two flared with energy as they attacked each other. Hurm Igrig stopped the recording in the middle of the battle.

'That's it!' shouted Bethany triumphantly (although without her ring her voice barely carried).

The jury perked up with interest.

Hurm Igrig strode into the centre of the court with an air of importance, sensing the shift in the atmosphere of the courtroom. 'As you are aware, your honour, I have been heading the investigation into Quinn and his accomplices. That investigation has involved surveillance of a highly specialised nature, often dangerous, often in the physical realm, and it has required the use of a cloaking form.' He bowed politely to the judge. 'If you would allow me, your honour?'

'Granted.'

Hurm Igrig removed his gown and wig, taking several paces forward and checking he had sufficient space around him. He muttered a series of phrases under his breath and made several precise gestures with his hands. His body shifted and jerked. He fell forwards on to his hands as his back rippled and stretched, his limbs lengthening into elegant paws. His lumpy, sagging face with its bulbous nose sprouted outwards and took on the sleek features of a cat. His black, silvery hair spread across his body, although the silver tips darkened into a fine black fur. And lastly, his bushy eyebrows retracted back into his face to reveal his eyes: two orbs of glowing orange.

Bethany's spirit body ran ice cold with fear. She was too astounded to fully understand what was happening. He had been tricking her all this time. He had been following her and trying to attack her with curses and now he had made her look guilty in front of the whole court. *This was all wrong. This was a waking nightmare. This was . . . this was . . .*

'I assumed the cloaking form of a cat in the physical realm so I could move around freely without appearing conspicuous. That way Quinn had no way of identifying me,' Hurm Igrig was saying. He flicked his tail at the recording. 'As you can see, my attack was not on Bethany but on the pooka, and was merely an attempt to arrest the culprit. Sadly, a failed attempt, as I had no back-up and had to flee the scene.'

Bethany managed to regain her ability to speak. 'It's you!' she shouted in an accusing tone. 'It's him,' she shouted at Flannigan, then at the judge. Without her ring, though, she had to yell at the top of her voice. 'He is the one that has been following me and attacking *me*. He's the one that's lied and twisted everything to make me look guilty. He's the demon! You have to listen to me.'

The judge banged his mallet harshly and fixed her with a withering look. 'Hurm Igrig is a high-ranking leprechaun,' he reminded her. 'Your comments are not only preposterous but ill-advised, and I think we have all heard enough of your stories.' He waved his hand at her. 'Tiny mouth,' he muttered.

'NO! YOU HAVE TO LISTEN TO ME!' Bethany made it to her feet and wrestled with the two guards that grabbed her arms. She felt a tingling, tickling sensation as her mouth shrank down in size and her voice became little more than a comical whisper. She shouted in a more frenzied manner, futilely, and tried to break free of the guards' grip, only for them to march her away.

'I think this concludes our business,' the judge decided. 'The jury will now consider its verdict.'

Bethany was led away, past Hurm Igrig who was already changing back to his leprechaun form, staring at her with his orange eyes and grinning victoriously. Flannigan appeared ashen and terrified, and behind him the jury could be seen already making its unanimous decision. Bethany felt tricked, betrayed and humiliated. In a tiny voice, she sobbed.

CHAPTER TEN

THE CLOCKWORK PRISON

Bethany was not aware of being taken away from the court or of being led back down the clockwork steps. She was not aware of Flannigan joining her, or standing in front of the hallway of revolving doors, or of the reassurances he was offering her. Her mind had become a dazed blank. She simply could not accept that any of this was happening. All she had wanted was a normal summer, a summer without anything remotely strange or threatening happening. Yet here she was, trapped in some freakish nightmare.

'Please,' Flannigan was saying to her in an urgent voice that finally registered. 'You have to pull yourself together. Trust me, things are not as hopeless as they seem. You *have* to pull yourself together.'

Gradually, Bethany became aware of herself. She realised what he meant. Her spirit body was becoming vague, drifting apart in fine wisps. It left the edges of her body looking faint and weak, and she tried to regain focus.

'Come on. You're stronger than this,' Flannigan said, sounding almost desperate.

She raised her head slightly to acknowledge his presence and he perked up. He grabbed her hand and placed the green jewelled ring back on to her finger. 'You left this behind,' he muttered. 'Now I know how it seems, but we'll get you out of this. You have to trust me.'

'Trust you?' Bethany exclaimed, glad to find her mouth had returned to its normal dimensions. 'You did absolutely nothing, Flannigan. You were no use to me whatsoever. You let Hurm Igrig make me look like a guilty liar. It couldn't have gone any worse if you had stood up and told the jury I was guilty yourself.'

'Look,' Flannigan said firmly. 'I didn't tell you this before, but I knew there was no way we could have won that court case. Hurm Igrig has never lost a case in his history and he is an incredibly powerful and highly respected leprechaun.'

'He lied, Flannigan. It's him. *He* is the demon. He is the one that has been manipulating this whole thing. I don't know how he has done it, but I know it's him. He's been attacking me as the cat, and now he has managed to make me look guilty in court. He's probably set this whole thing up to make Quinn look guilty too. We have to stop him.'

Flannigan looked doubtful. 'This complicates things a

great deal. He really is a very powerful leprechaun. You don't know what leprechauns that powerful can do. Are you absolutely sure that he is the demon?'

'Positive.'

'I don't know. There was talk of demon activity in the city. A few unexplained disappearances. A few rumours. But for something like that to have taken hold of Hurm Igrig, it would be almost unthinkable.' He scratched his chin. The gemstone on his ring flared with a brief white flame. 'We need to go back for the verdict,' he sighed.

It was sinking in how much trouble Bethany was in. She was separated from her body, she was in a city of strange spirits that hated her and she had been made to look guilty of a terrible crime. 'What will happen to me, Flannigan?'

'Well, that's what we're about to find out,' he said ominously.

In silence, they ascended the staircase to the courtroom. Bethany remained quiet as the guards marched her to an area in front of the judge's box, anticipating that the judge might use magic on her again if she started shouting. Flannigan stayed by her side, and she could sense Hurm Igrig looming behind her. The crowded auditorium rang with celebratory noise as the leprechauns talked and laughed with one other. The judge brought the court to order with a single strike of his mallet, prompting a respectful silence to fall.

'Jury, have you reached your verdict?' he asked.

Much to Bethany's surprise the entire crowd of

leprechauns took to their feet and spoke in unison. 'We have at that, your honour,' they all said.

The judge rearranged his wig, adopting an authoritative pose. 'And what is it?'

'Well, your honour,' the hundreds of voices replied. 'It seems to us that Bethany Chase is guilty on all counts.'

'Guilty,' the judge repeated. The crowd applauded and cheered with unrestrained joy. Bethany took a step forward to protest her innocence, but Flannigan put a hand gently on her shoulder to stop her. The judge banged his mallet once and the entire court was plunged into darkness. A single beam of light pierced the blackness and focused on Bethany.

'Bethany Chase, you have been found guilty of aiding a known criminal in the most heinous act – the act of stealing leprechaun gold. The repercussions of this crime may be dire, upsetting the very balance of reality we are sworn to protect. You have lied, cheated and deceived for your own ends, a crime that deserves the ultimate penalty – the removal of your soul. However, this is your first offence, and you are human *after all*, and it seems clear that you are not fully aware of your own actions. I therefore, with a great deal of leniency, sentence you to a period of indefinite detention in the leprechaun open prison for serious offenders.' He paused for dramatic effect, lowering his voice to a sombre tone. 'I only hope that eternity gives you time to reflect upon your crimes.'

'But . . .' Bethany wanted to speak.

The judge rapped his mallet one last time, very forcefully. There was the sound of uproarious applause. The floor fell from under Bethany's feet and there was a sudden whooshing noise as she found herself plunging through the darkness, with all the sounds of the courtroom rushing away from her. She came crashing down on to the floor of a stone room. Two leprechauns in uniform looked up at her, one stout and scruffy, the other thin and with a long sloping nose. They were both studiously examining a ghostly map of a labyrinth on a large table that occupied most of the room. They were laughing together at the points of light moving around it. They turned to Bethany, changing their manner to serious and official.

'Well, how about that. A human. And a living ghost. We don't get many of you through here,' the stout leprechaun remarked.

'Um, where am I exactly?' Bethany asked. Besides the ghostly map there was little else of note in the room.

'The leprechaun open prison,' the thin leprechaun with the sloping nose said. 'We're your guards, but really we're just here to help.'

'Name?' the stout guard asked.

'Bethany. Bethany Chase.'

'Indefinite or partial detention?'

'Oh . . . um . . .' Bethany had the brief idea of saying partial but noticed the guards were chuckling to themselves.

'Just our little joke. You're all indefinite. If you proceed through that door.' The thin guard with a sloping nose pulled a lever and a door swung open beside Bethany. A wisp of white mist curled from the opening. The guard ushered her forward. 'You're free to go if you can find the way out, but you're probably best just moving around lots and chancing upon it rather than actually looking for the thing. On the plus side, you have got for ever to find it!'

Bethany took several tentative steps forward through the opening. The door behind her slammed shut and she spun on her heels. She found she was looking at a stone passageway with several smaller passages leading off from it, and a thick white mist swirling across the floor. The doorway had completely vanished, as had the brief sound of the guards sniggering. Vague moans and murmurs echoed from somewhere far away.

'Hello?' she called out. 'Is there anyone else here?'

She heard several voices responding, but the sounds quickly turned into the sort of whispering made by someone muttering to themselves, or, more precisely, lots of people muttering to themselves. The fog coiled about her, forming brief shapes that seemed to reach out, things made from mist that pawed and grabbed and clawed at her. It was enough to get her moving. She walked down the passage and turned down the first entrance, moving along a twisting, turning route that led to a junction. She turned right and found herself wandering down another winding passageway, with several exits leading off it. Each passage was made from the same gigantic blocks of stone, arranged in such a way that it was impossible to get any sense of direction, and making it feel like she was lost in the vast ruins of a castle.

Bethany tried a simple plan of turning right at every junction she came to, in the hope that she would eventually find the edges of the maze, and that, at least, might help her get her bearings. This seemed to work well until she turned a corner and collided with a leprechaun in a red hat. His low, pinched face stretched into a sneer of disgust. 'Sorry,' Bethany said, as she tried helping the leprechaun up.

'Don't bother me,' he spat at her, pushing her hand away. He strode off purposefully.

She quickly followed him, desperate for any kind of company. 'I've only just got here,' Bethany explained. 'Maybe we could help each other find the way out.'

But the leprechaun hurried away so quickly and expertly that she lost him at the next turn and found herself staring at six identical stone passages, unsure of which one she had emerged from. As soon as she thought she had found her place and resumed her plan of turning right, there was a sudden clicking, clacking noise. The clockwork sound of gears and cogs turning and shifting ended with a loud grating sound as all the walls moved, spinning round, stones sliding closed over exits, walls shifting to reveal new routes.

'Oh!' Bethany said to herself. She heard a chorus of similar sighs and curses echoing across the maze, as if there were loads of other spirits like her who had just started making some sense of the maze, only to find it muddled again.

She had to admit it, Hurm Igrig had certainly put her in the right place if he wanted to get rid of her. The prison was as grim as a dungeon and she was beginning to realise how impossible it was going to be to escape it. It didn't help that every time she stopped to try and orientate herself, the mist would gather around her in thick, twisting folds. And it was more than a little disheartening that every spirit she saw rushed away from her at great speed. Only once did she get close enough to speak to another one of the inmates. A waspish, petrified leprechaun warned her off as she approached him at a junction. 'Keep moving. You'll be quicker on your own,' he said, racing off down a crooked passage.

'But it makes more sense if we help each other,' she called after him.

Alone, she wandered through the depths of the maze. It was difficult to know how long she spent threading her way through the mass of interconnecting passages, even with the regular turning and swivelling of the walls. It could have been minutes, days or weeks, as the passage of time seemed as convoluted as the layout of the prison. Sometimes it seemed that only a few moments passed before the walls shook and shifted position. At other times, it felt like an age had passed. All she was certain of was that she had still not found the perimeter.

The hopelessness of her situation gradually sank in. She was trapped here. Flannigan couldn't help her even if he wanted to. In fact, she was beginning to think that he had been manipulated as easily as she had by Hurm Igrig. He seemed incapable of standing up against the olderleprechaun and all his reassurances counted for nothing. It was a bleak thought. It meant that she was stuck in this prison with very little hope of escape. Somewhere, far away in the real world, Donovan was walking around in her body, impersonating her. And that meant Bethany's parents wouldn't even know she was missing.

She slumped to the ground where she stood, struck down by the realisation. Her spirit body felt unaccountably heavy. She wanted to sleep, to drift away and forget about all of this, even if it was just for a moment. She wanted to close her eyes and for it all to be over. As the mist gathered around her, she felt she was sinking into it, and that she could finally rest.

The maze made its strange clicking, clacking sound as it swung and slotted into a new position. Bethany peered up. Her head felt like cotton wool, vague and dreamy, and she barely noticed the figure passing by her from a freshly revealed passage. Whoever it was would no doubt run away from her anyway. Something with two heads, four arms and four legs approached. The two faces leaned down through the thickening layers of mist. They were the faces of two identical elderly ladies, made up from a ghostly blue light.

'Maggie-Maggie?' Bethany murmured, sure that she must be dreaming now.

'Bethany?' two voices asked simultaneously. They were the voices of the conjoined twin ghosts Bethany had last seen a year ago escaping the ruins of the Spellbound Hotel.

'Is that you, dearie?' the sisters asked.

'Maggie-Maggie.' Bethany smiled. Her thoughts were sluggish and muddled, and she wasn't quite sure whether the sisters were actually there or whether she had invented their presence to cheer herself up.

The sisters helped her up, though, brushing away the thick shrouds of mist curling round her, so they must have been real. 'Come on, dearie, you need to keep moving,' left-headed Maggie said. 'You're coming apart,' her sister added in a worried tone. Bethany could see what they meant. The definition of her body had become indistinct, as if patches of it were frayed, dispersing into the dim substance of the mist. It was as it had been after the court case. Obviously, if you became too distraught your spirit began to fade. Bethany wondered if she cared that much – fading away was better than walking around here for ever, wasn't it?

'What's happening? I feel strange.'

The sisters marched her forwards, down the nearest passage. The movement alone helped shift some of Bethany's grogginess. 'It's easy to lose your hope in this place,' right-headed Maggie told her. 'And once that happens you lose a sense of yourself. That's why you need to keep moving. Otherwise you'll end up coming completely undone.'

Bethany looked at the twisting, rippling forms of the mist. She shuddered as she began to come to her senses. 'Maggie-Maggie,' she said once more, but this time with a rising note of surprise in her voice. 'You're here! You're actually here!'

The sisters nodded. 'Of course we're here. Although we'd rather not be.'

'I mean, I never thought I would meet you again. Not after the hotel.' As Bethany moved down several crooked passages, the muddled thoughts cleared and she remembered where she was. She remembered the images she had seen in court of Maggie-Maggie involved with Quinn's robbery. 'I just can't believe it.' She felt the emotion rise up in her.

Right-headed Maggie held up her hands. Left-headed Maggie patted Bethany's shoulder soothingly. 'It's OK, dearie. Everything's fine.'

'It's just . . .' She let out a sigh and hugged the sisters. 'I thought I was alone.'

'We know,' the sisters reassured her. 'This place has that effect on you.'

Bethany broke her embrace and started walking forward again, keeping up a steady pace. 'What happened?' she asked. 'How did you end up here?'

'The prison?' right-headed Maggie asked. 'Or this city?' left-headed Maggie added.

'Both.'

'Well,' left-headed Maggie began. 'There were lots of ghosts left over after you destroyed the hotel. Your friend, Quinn, he found us and let us come to the Stolen City with him. Not many ghosts are allowed in the city so we took it as a compliment that we were invited. Quinn seemed to like us. Thought we'd done you a good turn in the hotel and wanted to repay the favour. That's how we ended up working for him.'

Right-headed Maggie shook her head with dismay. 'We wish we'd never got involved with him. We didn't know that he was going to steal the gold, dear. We just took him wherever he wanted to go in that walking chair. It came as a bit of a surprise, to be honest, when we found ourselves in the middle of all this mess. Now look at us.'

'I know,' Bethany replied. She told the ghost sisters everything that had happened to her, beginning with the appearance of Quinn in the real world, the black cat, and the leprechauns bringing her here.

'We were worried something like this might happen,' the sisters said once they had listened to her story. It was impossible to ignore the worried expressions they shared with one another. They stopped mid-stride and faced Bethany, clutching at her hands. 'It's the Jackomuss demon,' the sisters said together bluntly. 'It survived.'

'What? What do you mean?'

The sisters shrugged and shook their heads. 'Quinn was hunting it. He was working as a demon hunter here and he thought he'd found it,' right-headed Maggie said. 'That's what he was doing just before he stole the gold.'

'I knew it!' Bethany shouted out, feeling vindicated. 'I knew I was right. I saw the demon escape when the hotel fell apart. I knew it had to be involved. I told Flannigan, I told him.'

The ghost sisters didn't share Bethany's enthusiasm. They looked pensive and concerned. And it didn't take long for that feeling to sink into Bethany as well. 'Oh,' she murmured. 'Yes, I suppose that is bad. I suppose that's very bad indeed.'

The sisters nodded.

'So what happened?' Bethany asked.

'He tracked it down,' left-headed Maggie replied. Her sister elaborated. 'It was here, Bethany. It was somewhere in this city. And Quinn was close to finding it. He seemed to think that it was someone in the justice building.'

'Hurm Igrig,' Bethany muttered to herself.

'But that was when he decided to steal the gold. And that's when we ended up in here.' The sisters gestured at the gloomy maze.

'Do you think he took the gold to protect himself?' Bethany asked. If the demon was strong he would need all the power he could get to defeat it.

'He was sure the demon was building up its power again. And he thought it was planning revenge. On both you and him. So maybe.'

Bethany remembered the demon's capacity for nastiness and outright hatred, as if it could drain away all hope and happiness just by its presence alone.

Right-headed Maggie said, 'He was getting ready to warn you.'

'Maybe that's why he appeared in the physical realm,' Bethany said. 'For all the good it did him. The demon's succeeded as far as I'm concerned. I only hope Quinn is doing better.'

'All we know is that he left us here,' the sisters said

bitterly. 'It doesn't seem you can trust any of the spirits in this city. They're all devious.'

Bethany nodded glumly in agreement. 'I know. I thought I could trust Flannigan but he's abandoned me. It was almost like he wanted the court case to be over as quickly as possible.'

'We should keep moving,' the sisters said together, although their tone suggested that they felt equally defeated. Their main concern was to keep moving so that they did not end up dissolving in the white mists of the prison. Whenever the prison made one of its clicking, clacking changes, they could hear the other inmates cursing and felt their own frustration magnifying. They were led down dead ends, became lost in tangles of passages and followed long winding routes that returned them to an area that looked identical to a point they had passed an age ago.

'This is no good,' Bethany said. 'We'll never get out of here.' She fell on to the ground, letting the mists engulf her.

'Come on, now. It could be worse,' the sisters said.

'Could be worse? What could be worse than this prison?' Bethany said indignantly.

Right-headed Maggie shook her head. 'Oh, there are worse things than this. This is where you end up if they're lenient with you. I have heard about spirits who have had complete soul removal as punishment for their crimes. *Horrible.*'

Bethany, though, wasn't looking up at the sisters. She was squinting at the small dot glinting at her through the mist. A very faint, almost imperceptible flicker of green light issued from her ring. It also occurred to her now that the ring was on the wrong finger. Flannigan hadn't placed it on her index finger as he had done originally, but on her little finger. 'Look at this,' Bethany said, holding it up for the sisters to inspect.

'Oh,' the sisters said. 'You've still got your ring. That should have been confiscated in court.'

'Flannigan put it back on. Why is it glowing like that?'

The ghost sisters gave a curious, uncharacteristic laugh. 'Well, dear. He mustn't have given up on you completely.'

Bethany didn't understand.

Right-headed Maggie explained. 'The ring has a different property for every finger you put it on. If you wear it on your index finger on your right hand it is *Open*, and it will allow you access to the city and any restricted areas – sort of like a key. If you wear it on the ring finger of your left hand it is *Cast*, and you can use it to cast spells. Index finger of your left hand is *Loud*, to amplify your voice, left little finger is *Show*, so you can access memories, and right little finger is . . . hmmm, I think that's *Find*. But on no account place the ring on your right thumb. Ever.'

Bethany leaped to her feet. 'So you're saying that this will help us find our way out?'

'No, it's not *find* in that way. It's so others can find you if you get lost,' right-headed Maggie said. 'Sort of like a beacon that works by —' She was momentarily distracted as a gap appeared in the nearby wall. A door-shaped section swung open from one of the blocks of stone directly opposite them, revealing the guards' room Bethany had seen on entering the prison. The guards were involved in a struggle and were exchanging blasts of magic. It took Bethany a moment to recognise Pat and Seamus. They were disguised as women and were ducking and dodging to avoid the guards' attacks. The scene crackled with bursts of energy. Seamus leaped on to the shoulders of the stout, scruffy guard and wrestled him to the ground.

Pat checked the glowing light from the ring on his hand and quickly stuck his head out of the opening. Bizarrely, he had flowing red hair and long eyelashes. He must have used temporary magic to hide his beard as the enchantment was wearing off and whiskers were sprouting from his chin. 'Don't ask,' he said as soon as he saw Bethany.

'Is it her?' Seamus called after him.

'Aye, it's her,' he shouted back. 'And she's with the ghosts who helped Quinn.'

'Maggie-Maggie,' the ghost sisters reminded him.

'As you say.' Pat disappeared back into the room. There was a crash as Seamus managed to knock the stout guard out. The remaining guard, overpowered, held up his hands in surrender.

'I'm really not happy about this,' the guard protested feebly.

Pat took a step out of the doorway. 'Quick!' he shouted.

Bethany and Maggie-Maggie leaped into action, rushing through the entrance.

'Releasing prisoners,' the guard with the sloping nose said

in a disapproving tone. 'That carries a maximum penalty. They'll remove your souls for this.'

Seamus heaved the short, stout leprechaun through the doorway and dumped him unceremoniously on to the floor of the maze. With a few threatening hand gestures, he instructed the other one to follow.

'I'll give you one last chance to stop this nonsense, ladies,' the guard said. 'If you let me and my associate go, we'll say no more about this. How about that?'

Pat considered, scratching his chin as his beard grew more noticeable. 'Number one, we don't like jailors. Number two, we're not ladies. Good luck finding your way out.' His voice broke into a deranged cackle.

'I take it that's a no then?' the guard said quietly to himself as the door slammed shut on him.

Inside the guards' room, Pat and Seamus quickly removed the dresses to reveal white uniforms beneath. Maggie-Maggie had drifted towards the ghostly map of the prison, examining the points of light circulating through the maze of passages. Bethany stared at the leprechauns. 'You came back for me,' she said in amazement.

'Of course,' Seamus replied, offended. 'It was all part of the plan.'

'The plan?' she echoed.

Pat was checking the doorway. He signalled to Seamus who quickly took a quantity of dust from the pouch on his belt. He threw a handful over the ghost sisters and then a handful over Bethany. They glittered briefly, and Bethany felt her spirit body tingle as the powder came into contact with her. Her face stretched and altered shape. Across from her, Maggie-Maggie was also warping. The sisters' faces drooped like melting wax, then stretched forward into the exaggerated characteristics of a leprechaun. Large unsightly lumps appeared in patches across their foreheads.

'If anyone asks, you've sustained a magical injury and we're taking you to the hospital. Keep your faces covered. These disguises won't last long and any higher grade leprechauns will see right through them.'

Bethany was still struggling with the realisation that the leprechauns hadn't abandoned her after all. 'You planned all this?' she spluttered.

Seamus looked at her and grinned. 'Of course we planned it. Flannigan knew that there was no way you would win that court case. He knew you were being set up. So we thought we'd better spend our time a little more constructively. It's not easy gaining access to the guards' room, you know.'

'Wait. You're telling me Flannigan knew all along?' Her voice took on a hard edge. 'You're saying he let me suffer in court, knowing what was going to happen to me? Is that really what you're telling me?'

Seamus gave her a pleading look. 'Please don't be angry. There was no other way, really.'

She was furious now. 'Have you any idea how I felt? I was terrified! You couldn't have warned me? You couldn't have let me know what was going on?'

Pat raised his hands. 'Bethany, please. If you had known the plan it would have instantly aroused suspicions from the jury, from the judge, from Hurm Igrig. Your reactions would have been wrong. It would have been a dead giveaway. Now, you can be angry at us if you want to, but remember we're risking a lot coming here to save you.'

She felt a simmering rage but knew now was not the time to express it.

'And just so you know, it tore Flannigan up knowing that you were going to have to go through all of this. That's why he wanted to get through the court case so quickly,' Pat added. 'He didn't like the plan but there was nothing else we could do.'

'Even so . . .' Bethany muttered sulkily.

Seamus, listening to the ticking mechanism of the building surrounding them, moved impatiently. He seemed to have detected something urgent. 'We need to go. We don't have much time.'

Pat led the way. They walked briskly in single file up several flights of stairs, along corridors and through the lobby of the justice building. Bethany was terrified that they would bump into Hurm Igrig at any moment, but their route was mercifully free from other spirits. Only once did they stumble into a group of leprechauns gathered at the top of the steps on the outside of the building. Bethany and Maggie-Maggie ducked their heads as Pat and Seamus escorted them past the group.

'Let's hope it's not catching,' Seamus joked to the curious

leprechauns. The group all hurried off in the opposite direction.

Bethany and Maggie-Maggie were bundled on to a waiting chair – a large hairy-looking thing that must have been some type of bear. Flannigan was waiting in the front seat with a glowing pot perched beside him. He wore a serious, slightly guilty expression. 'I know you're probably angry at me right now,' he said. 'But I had to do what I had to do.'

Bethany was quiet for a moment. Then she said, 'You came back for me, Flannigan. That's the main thing.'

CHAPTER ELEVEN

FRIENDS IN SMALL PLACES

They made it to the Mineral Underground without incident and even managed to find an empty carriage. The leprechauns replaced their white uniforms with green ones. Flannigan had been quiet on their way there, obviously wanting to attract as little attention as possible. As soon as the train thundered upwards on its vertical path, though, his talk became animated and urgent.

'We're sending you back. It's the safest place for you, but then again, that's not really saying much. I tried to follow Hurm Igrig after the court case but I lost him at the Mineral Underground. He must've taken a train somewhere. Maybe back to your physical realm.'

Bethany nodded her head. 'Maybe to finish Quinn off.

Quinn was searching for the Jackomuss demon,' she told him. 'He thought it was in your city and that it was trying to seek revenge. He was sure the demon had worked its way into the justice building.'

The ghost sisters confirmed this with two curt nods of their heads. 'Just before he stole the gold,' left-headed Maggie added.

'It must have got Hurm Igrig. When could it have stolen his identity?'

The leprechauns shifted in their seats nervously. Flannigan's manner was grave. 'Hurm Igrig investigates all sorts of crimes, often before they happen. When we returned after being trapped in the hotel, it reflected badly on him. He should have noticed our disappearance sooner and he should have been aware of a major demonic event like that. Anyway, he was involved in the investigation afterwards. That's the only time he could have come into contact with the demon. The demon could certainly steal his powers and pose as him but it would be difficult. I've heard about a type of magic called mirror magic. Dark magic, terrible and cruel. The spirit being impersonated needs to be kept close by so the demon can drain their powers. It feeds off them slowly.'

'Quinn must have realised that it had got Hurm Igrig. I think that's why he took the gold. He came to the physical realm to protect me and try and fight it somewhere he had a chance,' Bethany said.

'Well, stealing that gold might bring its own problems,'

Flannigan commented in a disapproving tone. 'You need to get to Quinn and find out what he's got planned to get rid of the demon.'

She nodded. They both fell back into deep thought.

'Well, how about something to cheer you up in the meantime?' Pat said eventually to break the silence.

It took her out of her thoughts. The three leprechauns were grinning at her in a knowing way. Pat nudged Flannigan. 'Shall we give them to her now?' he asked.

'I suppose.' He reached his hand inside the pot. The contents responded with a shimmering pulse of light. 'You'll need all the help you can get if you confront the demon.'

'I don't need any help,' Bethany said boldly. She felt her resolve strengthening. 'I'm sick of being tricked and manipulated. I've had enough. I'm going to find Quinn and we're going to destroy that demon. And this time it's not going to escape.'

The change in Bethany's manner was so dramatic that all the leprechauns fell silent, staring at her with awe.

'Oh, right,' said Pat respectfully. 'I mean, you don't have to take any of this stuff if you don't want to but . . . well, why don't you look at it before you decide.' He removed something from the pot and handed it to her carefully.

She looked down at the object in her hand. It resembled a pair of glasses, although ones that seemed to be made from a fluid substance that was constantly shifting and re-forming. Even holding them in her hand was a struggle, as the glasses seemed to be constantly slipping out of her grip. Her interest was roused. 'What are these, exactly?'

'They're spirit glasses. Not much use now, but as soon as you're back in your body they will help you see the spirit realm. You'll be able to spot any strong spirits – like a demon – from a good way off. You've been easy prey up until now, but these will help give you an advantage.'

'Hmmm. Actually, that does sound kind of useful,' she conceded. 'Maybe a little help wouldn't be so bad.'

Pat grinned. 'That's more like it.'

'Give me your arm.' Flannigan scooped out something from the pot that writhed and squirmed like a snake, although one formed entirely out of strange symbols, like the magical inscriptions Donovan had drawn on to bits of paper in her bedroom in the physical realm. Reluctantly, Bethany held out her hand as the word-snake coiled up her arm and bonded with the fabric of her spirit body, resembling some sort of tattoo made up of letters from an ancient language.

'This is a protection spell. It should deflect a magical attack, even a strong one. But once it's used up, that's it.'

She nodded.

'Lastly . . .' The leprechaun removed a small, swirling sphere of gold. Pat, Seamus and Flannigan all stared at it longingly, adoringly, obsessively. For a moment Bethany thought that Flannigan might not pass it over after all. 'Leprechaun gold forms many things. This piece is pure luck. And let's be honest, you really need some good luck right now.'

Flannigan dropped it on to Bethany's outstretched hand. She held it in her palm for several moments. Gradually, it began to melt into her hand, sending a flood of gilded light through her spirit body. She felt a wonderful warm sensation, followed by an overwhelming wave of hope and confidence. *It was going to be OK. She was going to find Quinn. They were going to stop the demon together.*

'Dearie, you look . . .' Maggie-Maggie examined Bethany with amazement. 'You look dazzling!' the sisters said together.

'Thank you, Flannigan,' Bethany said. 'And you, Pat and Seamus. I'm sorry I doubted you. I —'

But Bethany was cut short as the train burst free from its tunnel. It passed over London in a wide arc. An unusual amount of activity was stirring in the adjoining carriages and it didn't take Bethany long to see what was concerning the other leprechauns on the train. She peered out of the window to look at the sight of the city below them. The spirit realm of the city no longer glowed with its rich mixture of light and colour. Instead, a vast dark stain hung over it like polluted black smog, with specks of gold scattered throughout it. The inhabitants of London were caught up in this substance, no longer the vivid points of light Bethany remembered seeing on her first trip, but dim smudges of light underneath the spreading darkness. She wondered how long she had been away for things to change so much.

The leprechauns and Maggie-Maggie were pressed up against the windows.

'This is bad,' Flannigan stated in a sober tone.

'Catastrophic is what it is,' Seamus added.

'And whatever is beyond catastrophic,' warned Pat.

Flannigan turned to Bethany, 'This is what happens when a spirit uses too much gold in the physical realm. All that magic . . . it is warping reality out of shape.'

It did indeed look disastrous. There were strange cracks and tears appearing in the spirit realm, as if it was crumpling under an enormous strain. The origin of that strain was situated in a part of London Bethany didn't recognise. Something dark and powerful was drawing in a steady stream of light. It was like looking at water being sucked down a plughole, except this was the spirit energy of an entire city slowly being drained to a single point.

'It looks like something is about to break,' Bethany said.

'It is,' the leprechaun replied ominously. 'Reality is in danger of collapsing. And if it does, the two separate realms will crash together, causing the laws of each to break down. Nothing would make sense any more. Imagine if everyone in the physical realm could see everything in the spirit realm. And imagine if everything in the spirit realm became as real and solid as everything in the physical realm. Chaos. Disaster.'

'Oh.'

'Uh-huh.'

'Hmmmm.'

The train moved more erratically than ever, trying to avoid the streaks and cracks highly visible in the spirit realm.

As it curled sideways in an effort to avoid a tear, part of one of the rear carriages connected with it and was ripped apart. There was a chorus of screams as the train dived down but, luckily, it was manoeuvring itself so that it came to a skidding halt outside Bethany's bedroom window at her aunt's house.

A gigantic version of Bethany stood above the windowsill, frowning at them angrily. A bell sounded *ding-ding* and the leprechauns leaped into action, scuttling out of the train and hurrying down on to the edge of the bed.

'You were away too long,' Donovan said, although his voice was indistinguishable from Bethany's.

'Why, how long has it been?' Bethany asked, looking at Donovan then Flannigan.

'It's been about three weeks your time,' Flannigan muttered.

'Three weeks?'

Pat, Seamus and Flannigan were all looking back at the carriages, worried that the passengers would notice them. Luckily, the other leprechauns were too concerned with the damage to the train to notice what was going on. Nevertheless, they moved extremely quickly, shifting the pot into place and aiming it at Bethany's body. She dived into the stream of gold and was fired back into her body. But as she struck the edge of her physical self, she rebounded off.

'I told you. You've been too long,' Donovan scolded them angrily. 'I've started bonding with the body.'

Dazed, Bethany was helped up by Pat, who led her back

to the pot. 'We better try that one more time,' he suggested nervously.

She didn't know what she was going to do if she couldn't get back in her body. 'You told me it was safe,' she said to Flannigan in a desperate tone.

The leprechaun fidgeted and gestured for her to dive back into the pot. She did so, this time hurtling forward and connecting violently with her physical body. She could feel its resistance and was sure she would bounce off it once more, but Donovan managed to heave himself free from it, so that Bethany was sucked back into her physical body.

'See,' Flannigan said, shrugging his shoulders. 'I told you it was all fine.'

Donovan looked as unhappy about all of this as Bethany felt. 'I can see you have some luck,' he remarked to her. 'You'll need it. Something has gone wrong here. I tried to stop your parents, but they are too easily influenced by Quinn's magic. I don't know what he's doing, but he's become much more powerful over the last few weeks. You'll need to be careful.'

'Don't worry about me.' Bethany looked at him. 'You know, these spirit glasses really work,' she said, impressed. The spirit glasses had enlarged with her body and she could see the leprechauns clearly.

She watched as Flannigan addressed Maggie-Maggie. 'I think it's best if you stay here,' he suggested. 'You're a fugitive now and you need to keep away from leprechauns. It won't be long before your escape becomes common knowledge.'

'I suppose so,' right-headed Maggie agreed hesitantly. Left-headed Maggie added, 'We could keep an eye on Bethany. If that's OK, dearie?'

'Of course.' Bethany nodded.

Pat and Seamus sprang back into action, using their pot to enlarge Maggie-Maggie back to her normal size. The ghost sisters didn't seem to enjoy this shift in size, having spent so long in the leprechaun city. They swayed to and fro unsteadily.

'Listen,' Flannigan said. 'We are going to try and find Hurm Igrig. You need to stop Quinn using any more of that gold, whatever his reasons are. This reality is under a huge amount of pressure. He's in danger of causing it to collapse completely.'

'OK,' Bethany replied. She watched as the leprechauns ran to the train. 'Be careful,' she called after them.

'And you,' Flannigan replied.

They hurried on board the Mineral Underground and the train shot away at high speed, as if it was desperate to escape. In moments, it was nothing more than a blur against the night sky.

'Well,' left-headed Maggie sighed. 'Looks like we're free. Maybe the leprechauns aren't so bad after all.'

'Yeah,' Bethany murmured, thinking of the clockwork prison and the endlessly convoluted passages. They could still have been trapped if it wasn't for Pat, Seamus and Flannigan, and she realised how grateful she was for their help. Out of habit, she checked the window for any signs of the cat, then just as quickly realised that it would no longer be looking for her. Now, at least, she had an advantage over the demon. She had the element of surprise. Her gaze strayed to the outside world and she noticed again the streaky patches where the spirit realm was breaking under the strain. She just had to make sure she made it to Quinn quickly. 'Although I think we have a whole new set of problems to deal with,' she said.

Maggie-Maggie surveyed the nearby houses. The ghost sisters appeared fainter now that they were their normal size, and Bethany was sure it was not some fault in the spirit glasses. The sisters looked weak, casting a thin blue impression in the spirit realm. When Bethany tried taking the glasses off – a feeling like removing a wisp of smoke from her face – she couldn't see any hint of the sisters in the real world. *That might be useful*, she thought. 'We will start searching for Quinn first thing in the morning,' she told Maggie-Maggie. 'I need to rest for a moment.'

She could make out the sisters replying, but their voices were extremely distant, as if the glasses also helped Bethany register spirit sounds as well. 'I'm so tired,' Bethany said, falling sideways on to the mattress. Her physical body felt huge and heavy but it was her exhausted spirit that forced her into a deep, impenetrable sleep.

'I'll just keep watch, dearie,' she thought she heard one of the sisters say.

CHAPTER TWELVE

STRANGE DAZE

Sunshine streamed through the bedroom window and, before she was fully conscious, Bethany felt as if she had woken up to a blissfully normal morning. That contentment lasted only for a few brief moments before she leaped up with a start, remembering all that had happened. *I've got to get moving. I've got to think of a plan. Everyone's in danger.*

She was up and out of bed in a flash, forgetting about Maggie-Maggie and the spirit glasses. Dashing into the bathroom, she splashed cold water on her face, glad to feel herself solid again. She barely noticed the tubes of Quinn toothpaste, or the boxes of Quinn hair dye, or the range of Quinn make-up, all crowding the bathroom cabinet. She bounded downstairs, leaping over the cats and dogs lolling in the hallway, only faintly acknowledging the stacks of large cardboard boxes along one wall. The sound of her mother singing away to herself greeted her as she rushed into the kitchen.

'Mum!' Bethany ran over to her mother and instinctively hugged her. 'I missed you. I —' She stopped, noticing how wide her mother felt, and for a bizarre moment thought she had mistakenly hugged a stranger.

'Morning, Bethany,' Mrs Chase smiled.

The person in front of Bethany was definitely her mother, but she was completely transformed. In the three weeks Bethany had been away Mrs Chase had put on so much weight that her belly stuck out. Numerous Quinn products had taken their toll. She had a wide, grinning mouth of brilliantly white teeth. Her hair had turned from a dark red to a bright pink and had been cut back and teased into a quiff. She must have also been using some sort of cream on her face, as her skin had an unnatural quality to it that left it smooth and shiny. She was even wearing a black bodysuit just like Quinn's. By far the strangest aspect to her, though, was the way that she shone with a dazzling light. This, perhaps, explained why the cats and dogs were keeping their distance from her.

Bethany gawped at her mother, unable to hide her shock. 'Mum, you look . . . *different*,' she said.

'Thank you,' Mrs Chase smiled, taking it as a compliment and giving a mock curtsy. 'I think it must be the new eyeliner.'

'Yeah . . . that's it . . . new eyeliner.' Bethany found herself backing away from her mother, only to stumble over a pile of boxes on the floor and fall clumsily to the ground.

'I really am blessed,' Mrs Chase commented in a dreamy voice. 'Quinn is a miracle worker.'

Bethany lifted the flap of the nearest cardboard box to reveal the contents. It was full to the brim with packages of Quinn moisturising cream. *Will make you feel like a different person!* the slogan declared. The boxes, Bethany realised, were everywhere; they were stacked in tall piles behind the door, they lined the hallway, they were balanced on top of cupboards in the kitchen. As she checked through them she found a mixture of toothpastes, i-Stink aftershaves, sweets, and pink hair dye. It dawned on Bethany what had been going on while she had been away.

'You're selling this stuff?' she exclaimed. 'You're actually selling it now?'

Mr Chase entered the room at that moment. 'Sell it?' he beamed. 'This stuff practically sells itself.'

He was, much to Bethany's horror, similarly unrecognisable. His smile stretched most of the way across his face and his hair was identical to Mrs Chase's. As he walked into the kitchen an intense pine-scented cloud of aftershave followed him.

'The more we sell, the more we can buy, and that means our chances of finding the winning ticket go up,' Mr Chase added excitedly. He ruffled Bethany's hair as he wandered into the kitchen. He helped himself to a bowl of Quinn brand cereal. The contents bubbled and frothed as he added the milk and made a brief laughing noise.

'Oh, don't,' Mrs Chase complained. 'You'll just get my hopes up.'

'What ticket?' Bethany said, edging over to the table to look at the newspaper.

'You know, the ticket everyone is after. A day out with Quinn. A chance to meet him in his own house and spend some time with the great man himself!' Mr Chase wagged his finger at his daughter. 'You know, I'm sure we had this conversation the other day.'

Bethany blushed slightly. 'Um, yeah, that's right . . . I forgot,' she replied. She smiled and saw, with some relief, that her father was too preoccupied by his breakfast to pursue it any further. *What was happening? Why was Quinn doing this?* She was horrified at the state of her parents and that Quinn, her friend, the one she had defended in court, was behind all this. *Had all that leprechaun gold caused him to lose his mind?*

Bethany seized the newspaper perched on the edge of the table. She quickly flicked through the articles. The amount of pictures and stories involving Quinn was staggering. He was shown at film premieres, handing out trophies at major sporting events, and sitting on the judging panel for talent shows. *It was all wrong.* She flung the paper back down in disgust.

Aunt Bess strode into the room and her appearance, much to Bethany's relief, hadn't changed at all. Even more reassuring was her look of pure and utter disdain at the boxes of Quinn merchandise. Without thinking, Bethany flung her arms round Aunt Bess. 'You're normal,' she blurted out.

'Bethany,' Aunt Bess exclaimed, initially taken aback by this gesture, then brightening a little at the affection. She looked at Bethany carefully, frowning a little. 'You seem different today. A bit more . . . yourself.'

Bethany jerked backwards instinctively, as if she had just been caught up to no good.

'Morning, Bess,' Mr Chase greeted. 'Would you like to try some of this cereal? It's a specially formulated mixture of superfoods and relaxed fats designed to give the perfect —'

'No,' Aunt Bess said to her brother bluntly. 'A dippy egg and soldiers will suffice for me, thank you.'

Mr and Mrs Chase didn't seem to notice Aunt Bess's frustrated mood. She became quiet and terse in response to Bethany's parents' constant chatter. Almost all their conversation was about Quinn and how wonderful he was and what wonders his products performed. This did not impress Aunt Bess in the slightest.

Bethany quickly ate some toast before sneaking back to her bedroom. The grogginess had cleared from her head since first waking up and she had to check on Maggie-Maggie. She examined her empty bedroom and momentarily wondered if the ghosts had left during the night. 'Maggie-Maggie?' she called quietly.

There was a faint stirring in the air and Bethany felt something brush against her face. The spirit glasses dropped over her eyes – a strange, ticklish sensation like walking into a cobweb. She found herself suddenly able to see the ghost sisters standing directly in front of her, adjusting the glasses they had just placed over her eyes.

'These might help,' left-headed Maggie smiled. 'You dropped them last night when you fell asleep.'

'Thanks.' In truth, the glasses felt a little disorientating, as the ghostly landscape of the spirit realm was superimposed over the real world. 'Weird,' she muttered. 'Right, we need to get going. Something bad is happening here. If we're going to find Quinn we need to do it quickly.'

'We know!' the sisters exclaimed together. Left-headed Maggie added, 'We've already had a look around.' Right-headed Maggie gestured at the spirit glasses. 'You need to see it through those. Come on, dear. We'll have a walk and show you what we mean.'

'But what if someone sees you?' Bethany asked, concerned.

'No one can see us except you,' left-headed Maggie told her. 'It's only ghosts that want to be seen that can be seen. Really, dearie, we would've thought you knew that by now.'

Bethany laughed sheepishly before following the sisters downstairs. They could move a lot quicker than Bethany as they could, with a little effort, pass through solid objects, finding it easier to simply drift through the front door rather than wait for it to be opened.

Outside in the street people were leaving their houses to get to work. Virtually everybody was a Quinn lookalike, with their dyed pink hair, their wide gleaming grins, and their black bodysuits. This alone was strange enough, but viewed through the spirit glasses the scene took on an alarming aspect. The Quinn products were laced with leprechaun gold and Bethany could see it clearly as hundreds of tiny hooks that were sticking to people's spirits. *That was why people were attracted to his products.* The golden hooks were drawing off the light from the spirit bodies of everyone Bethany saw and causing black clouds to form as a result. A middle-aged businessman talking on his mobile phone passed her, and his face was almost completely obscured by a dark stain.

'See?' Maggie-Maggie said.

Bethany turned towards them. This was an equally strange sight, viewing the ghost sisters in the middle of a suburban street with people walking past her and, in one case, directly through her. 'This is . . . bad. Something is wrong with all of this. We should check the shops. See if it's like this everywhere.'

As Bethany was addressing the ghost sisters Aunt Bess's neighbour, the short, elderly woman that Bethany kept glimpsing through her bedroom window, stepped out from her house. Bethany was, to all intents and purposes, addressing thin air, and the neighbour gave a frightened smile before edging away, a smile that was ludicrously wide.

Bethany opened her mouth to explain, thought better of it and headed off in the opposite direction towards the shops, with the sisters following behind her obediently. In every street she ran down she was alarmed to see the same thing. Almost everyone she encountered had a Quinn look to them, with a black cloud hovering over them. This was at its worst by the line of shops on the main street, the windows glimmering with the charmed Quinn merchandise, the steady traffic of pedestrians generating a thick, gloomy mist above their heads. Even the images of Quinn on adverts were riddled with the tiny golden hooks, explaining why the pictures had such a draw on people.

'This isn't Quinn,' she told the sisters, whispering so that no one else would think she had gone mad. It reminded her of one thing and one thing only: this was just like the cursed magic she had witnessed in the spirit hotel. The hairs on the back of her neck stood up. 'This is the work of the demon.'

The magic was everywhere, causing black clouds to hover over individuals, which in turn were amassing to form the heavy smog that filled the spirit realm. A steady trickle of light was running in rivulets and courses between these dark clouds, draining towards a point somewhere on the other side of London. Bethany wondered how long it would take them to follow that light. It would, after all, lead to the source of this cursed magic, which in turn would lead them to Quinn, or the demon, or both.

'Maybe the demon has got to him already,' left-headed Maggie murmured. Her sister shook her head, baffled by it all.

'We need to get to him and quickly. I think I've figured it out wrong.' Bethany felt a tingling sensation from her ring and decided to get back to the house as quickly as possible. She hurried along streets, dodging Quinn lookalikes, as Maggie-Maggie followed behind her. She noticed the two boys she had first seen with the same tracksuits eating the firework sweets. Now they were large and plump in their black bodysuits, and both were boasting identical pink haircuts. She hid behind the large overgrown hedge of Aunt Bess's house as the two boys passed, and quickly ducked into the garden as her parents, by chance, were emerging from the front door.

'Bethany, there you are!' her mother said.

'Can you please not wander off without letting either us or your aunt know where you've gone?' Mr Chase asked. He was probably trying to make a serious point, but his stretched, smiling mouth made it impossible for him to sound angry.

Bethany nearly yelped at the sight of them. Viewed through the spirit glasses, they looked nightmarish. The tiny golden hooks completely covered them and were soaking up the light from their spirits, leaving black stains so thick across their faces that only their fake grins were visible. She had to fight her initial instinct to ask them if they were OK, as it was very clear that they were very far from being OK. Some of the golden hooks, having soaked up enough energy, were channelling that light so that it drifted away in the spirit realm. 'Are you . . . are you going out?' she asked in a high, uncertain voice.

'*Bethany*. We're doing our door-to-door sales,' Mrs Chase

explained. 'We *have* been doing this every day for the last week now,' her mother reminded her in a gently mocking tone.

'Yeah, I know . . . I just . . . thought you might be doing it later today,' she said feebly.

'Silly,' Mr Chase laughed. 'You would forget your own head at the moment if it wasn't screwed on.'

'We'll be back for lunch,' her mother said as she walked away.

Her parents trundled up the street, lugging a packed suitcase on wheels after them. Bethany rushed indoors and heaved a sigh of relief as soon as the door was closed. She didn't notice her aunt standing in the hallway, cleaning out one of the bird cages, and flinched when Aunt Bess addressed her. 'I'm sure they will snap out of it soon,' she said reassuringly.

Flustered, Bethany tried to regain her composure, then realised there was no point. 'They're selling it,' she said, dazed. 'They're actually selling it.'

Aunt Bess nodded, as if acknowledging something unspoken. 'Actually, I think they're still buying and using more than they can sell.' Her face took on an expression of disdain and she surveyed the boxes crowding the hallway. 'They're determined to find that winning ticket. They go through loads of packets looking for it.' She tutted in dismay.

Bethany fell into a gloomy silence. A thought crossed her mind. 'Why aren't you affected by it? You know, by all this Quinn stuff?' she asked. It was almost as if her aunt was not only unaffected by the charmed items, but actively repelled them.

Aunt Bess hadn't thought about this, though, and shrugged her shoulders. 'I don't know, really. I mean . . .' She paused to consider something. 'I've never really followed the crowd, so to speak, and neither did my mother. Maybe it's something to do with the Chase women. Your father's probably not mentioned it, but the Chase family tree has a bit of a history.'

'Really?'

'Oh, yes. Your great-great-grandmother liked to be referred to as a "white witch". She was very odd, apparently. And your great-aunt thought she could speak to ghosts. Yes, it always affects the women for some reason. I think it's why I sometimes have these funny feelings about things.'

Bethany didn't dare look at Maggie-Maggie for fear her aunt might detect their presence. 'Funny feelings?'

Her aunt's face screwed up with concentration. 'Yes. Like all this Quinn stuff. There's just something about it . . . something odd. It doesn't feel right.'

Bethany didn't know what to say. It was as if her aunt picked up on the true nature of the cursed products. *She must be sensitive to things in the spirit realm*, Bethany thought.

'Anyway, maybe that's where you get it from.' Aunt Bess smiled affectionately at Bethany. 'Although your father doesn't seem to have been as lucky,' she joked drolly.

Bethany laughed along with her aunt politely, then stopped suddenly.

'Bethany?'

An idea struck her. 'Lucky,' she murmured. 'Of course! Luck. All I need to do is use it.'

'Bethany, are you sure you're all right?'

A wild expression had crossed Bethany's face and she giggled uncontrollably. Maggie-Maggie hovered by her side, fretfully wringing their hands. 'What is it, dearie?' left-headed Maggie asked in a whisper.

'I've got to concentrate,' she said seriously. She positioned herself so she was standing over the boxes. She closed her eyes, held her arms out and spread her hands. She tried to let herself be guided by her instinct.

'What are you doing?' Aunt Bess asked, looking at her as if she had lost her mind.

'Well, I think I've just realised something.' Bethany thought of the leprechauns' gold that Flannigan had given her. She thought she could feel it now, gently flowing through her. It made her lean down and plunge her hand into a box on her right. There was no way to explain to her aunt that she had been given pure luck by some leprechauns. 'It sounds mad but . . . I'm lucky. That means if anyone's going to find that ticket it's going to be me.'

Her aunt scoffed at this notion with a dismissive but good-natured laugh. 'I don't wish to dash your hopes, but I hardly think that's going to happen.'

Bethany rustled through the full box, searching out something that seemed to be attracting her hand. In a single decisive move she delved her hand deep down and pulled out a box of Quinn hair dye. She ripped it open, grinned

181

triumphantly and removed a card decorated with a large golden *Q* on the front of it, as if stamped with a golden seal. As she turned it over, some device in the card was activated and it played the pre-recorded sound of applause and a spoken message. 'CONGRATULATIONS! YOU ARE THE WINNER! CONGRATULATIONS! YOU ARE THE WINNER! CONGRATULATIONS!'

'See,' Bethany said. Her aunt, the ghost sisters and the collection of animals gawped at her in amazement.

'How on earth did you . . . ?' But Aunt Bess thought better of wanting to know how Bethany had found the ticket. Wearily, she sighed, and strolled towards the kitchen. 'I'll put the kettle on,' she said simply.

As Bethany waited for her parents to return home she tried to reassure Aunt Bess that finding the ticket had been a complete stroke of luck. Aunt Bess wore the confused expression of someone resigned to the fact that the world had stopped making sense.

When Mr Chase stepped through the door, Bethany ran forwards, clutching the ticket in her hand. 'Dad, you won't believe it,' she said.

Her father looked at her and smiled, but she could see something wasn't quite right. His teeth no longer shone so brilliantly and his smile no longer stretched so widely. His hair was bedraggled and dry as straw. Mrs Chase was no better, with blemished skin and heavy bags under her eyes. Not to mention the awful smell that issued from both of them as if they had fallen into a sewer. The magic of Quinn's products, so it seemed, was wearing off quickly. Viewed through the spirit glasses, the golden hooks had gone, but had left a dark stain behind that was larger than the one Bethany had seen on them that morning.

'Just give me one moment,' Mr Chase said with an edge of desperation.

'We just need to top up,' Mrs Chase said in a falsely cheery voice.

They both rushed upstairs to the bathroom and Bethany followed. She could hear them applying the pastes and creams and sprays and ointments. There was something unnerving in their hungry, greedy expressions. When they reappeared moments later, renewed and refreshed, she could see that the fresh layer of magic was working on them.

'How often do you need to do that?' she asked. 'You know, keep applying that stuff?'

Her parents were momentarily thrown by this. 'It's rude to ask too many questions,' her father stated.

'Does it wear off faster every time?' Bethany said, with a sudden inkling into how the magic might be working.

This, she could see, made both her parents furious. Mrs Chase opened her mouth as if she were about to tell her daughter off. Bethany waved the ticket in front of their faces. 'I have something,' she announced. 'I found this in one of the packets.'

Mr and Mrs Chase frowned doubtfully for a moment. They examined the ticket as if they weren't entirely sure what it was. When it dawned on them that it was the winning ticket that they had been hoping to find they nearly fell over with shock. 'Is . . . is th-this what I th-think it is?' stammered Mr Chase.

'Yes,' Bethany said.

Her parents burst into shrieks of joy. They began to laugh and cheer, holding each other and jumping up and down on the spot, waving the ticket above their heads victoriously. 'We've won,' they shouted in disbelief. Then more victoriously, 'WE'VE WON!!'

Bethany thought she saw tears in her mother's eyes and realised just how much they had fallen completely under Quinn's magic. It gave her a chill. She knew, whatever had happened, whatever was creating this cursed magic, she was finally going to get some answers. She could sense she was closing in on Quinn and the demon.

CHAPTER THIRTEEN

SURPRISE APPEARANCE

When Mr and Mrs Chase finally calmed down, they read out the details on the back of the winning ticket. It instructed them to ring a phone number and give the correct code written on the card. They did this immediately, and were told that a car would arrive for them in the morning to take them to Quinn's personal residence to enjoy a day of 'luxury pampering and a full Quinn makeover'. This made them dizzy with excitement.

Bethany, however, was feeling more and more apprehensive. She retreated to the safety of her room to discuss things with Maggie-Maggie. 'Well, at least we've got a way to get to Quinn now. And I think we're going to find the demon there too,' she said. 'I'm going to need your help. Hopefully we're not too late.'

As the room was so small the sisters were standing in the centre of the bed, their legs appearing submerged into the mattress. But Bethany was staring through them, out of her bedroom window and into the window of the neighbour's house. The elderly lady was there with her husband, peering back. It must have looked like Bethany was talking away to herself again. Annoyed, she jumped on to the bed – causing Maggie-Maggie to dodge out of the way – and pulled the curtains shut, exclaiming, 'I'm normal, I'm completely normal!' This caused her to lose her balance, falling sideways and knocking a pile of suitcases over.

'Is everything all right, dearie?' the sisters asked.

Bethany was covered in an avalanche of old photo albums, broken ornaments and dusty bric-a-brac. She shook herself free and groaned. As she sat up her hand fell on a small box. She glanced at it, recognising it as the empty box Quinn had given her in the car park. It glimmered brightly as she viewed it through her spirit glasses. She quickly opened it and found there was a leprechaun ring like the one Flannigan had given her. This one, though, was decorated with a cluster of pink gems.

'Oh,' Maggie-Maggie said, seeing it. 'Where did you get that from?' left-headed Maggie asked, while her sister pointed at the arrangement of pink gems and declared, 'That's Quinn's.'

'What?' Bethany said, sitting up.

'I recognise that. That was the ring Quinn used to wear,' right-headed Maggie explained.

Bethany looked at it. She removed her spirit glasses and, like Maggie-Maggie, it completely disappeared. She dropped her glasses back over her eyes and examined it closely. She tried picking it up. It felt strange, as if it had no substance at all, and was like grabbing a piece of smoke. 'But why would he give me a ring?'

'Could I have a look at that?' right-headed Maggie asked, reaching for the ring.

'Sure,' Bethany said, letting right-headed Maggie take it from her palm.

The ghost sister placed it on the little finger of her left hand. She frowned. 'Hmmm. That's strange, it's not showing its memories to me. Here, you try. If he gave it to you he might have charmed it.'

She took the ring and placed it on the little finger of Bethany's left hand. The pink gems glinted brightly as they attached to her spirit. She felt a tingling sensation. 'I think it's working,' she said excitedly.

'Twist the ring to the right or left to go back and forth. And pull it off your finger if you need to stop it. Oh, and —'

Bethany wasn't listening, though. She had just found herself immersed in Quinn's memories. The room, the house and Maggie-Maggie slipped away. In its place were the ruins of the Spellbound Hotel. It was a bizarre experience, feeling as if she had been dropped into the centre of the ghostly recordings made by the ring, with the outline of Quinn's body hanging over her own in a thin coat of light, and a wide sphere of activity projected around her.

She followed Quinn's gaze as he stood in the spirit realm examining the tattered remnants of the hotel and, in particular, a large oval mirror lying on the ground by his feet. The sight of it sent chills down Bethany's spine. A year ago, when she had left the spirit realm after destroying the hotel, she had seen the Jackomuss demon escaping from this place. Her last vision had been of a black flame emerging from this mirror and flying off. Now she was looking at it again, through Quinn's eyes, as he looked at his own reflection and a black scorch mark on the surface of the mirror.

'Hmmff. Anything of note?' grumbled a leprechaun walking towards him.

Quinn turned and acknowledged Hurm Igrig. Behind him, groups of leprechauns were investigating the scene, scouring the area and picking through the scattered remains of the hotel. A few pieces of the cursed magic had not fully dissolved – some pots and pans from the kitchen, as well as a couple of menus from the restaurant – and they examined them with interest. The leprechauns tested them with their own magic and the objects seemed to twitch and convulse like something partially alive.

'Quite a mess,' Hurm Igrig commented. 'It looks like a hybrid spirit controlled by a demon. Very dangerous, and, really, a massive oversight on our part. It could have broken the integrity of this reality if it had become any more powerful. Thank you, Quinn. We leprechauns owe you a debt. Frannigan has filled me in on some of your and —' he consulted his notepad '— Bethany Chase's exploits. I must say I am impressed. Quite a tale.'

Quinn giggled uncontrollably at this and had to slap a hand over his mouth to calm himself down.

Hurm Igrig frowned. 'Yes. Well, we'll conduct a clean-up operation and make a full report. I don't think we'll find much, by the look of things. The giant has gone. There are a few confused ghosts still haunting the area, but we might be able to put some of them to use in the city.'

The pooka coughed and tapped the mirror with his foot.

Hurm Igrig peered at it and harrumphed irritably. He leaned in close, switching his ring to his left hand so that a beam of light projected on to the mirror, magnifying the area it shone on. He aimed it on the scorch mark, revealing a creeping black substance. He adjusted the ring to increase the magnification. The black substance was made up from hundreds of tiny black flames, wriggling in a slow, drowsy motion. 'Residual traces of a type three demon,' Hurm Igrig concluded. 'Very weak, it appears. You think this has some bearing on the incident here?'

Quinn nodded.

'Well, if you think so,' Hurm Igrig replied in a tone that suggested he was deeply unconvinced. 'It was my understanding that the demon involved was destroyed.' He sounded annoyed, but tried to brush his doubts away and appear polite. 'I have just the chap, though. Gurdo Erlstan. One of our demon hunters. Excellent tracking skills.' He gestured to a nearby leprechaun. 'Gurdo, come over, please.'

A leprechaun in a pale blue uniform strode over. He had a serious face with a long, white moustache that hung downwards in two sharp points. He nodded at Quinn before examining the mirror with interest, viewing it through a coloured monocle that must have had similar powers to Hurm Igrig's ring.

The senior leprechaun stood upright. 'As a precautionary step, I would like you to find any trace of this demon, Gurdo. See if it has any connection with what happened here. We'll contain any residue or remains that you find.'

Gurdo Erlstan nodded, swapping the monocle as he scanned the area, already following a trail only he could see.

'Well, if there is anything, Gurdo will find it,' Hurm Igrig said, his eyebrows knitting together. 'But I really feel that this matter is largely closed. Trust me, that demon has gone for good.'

Quinn stared at the mirror. The black scorch marks hung over his reflection and a low, worried sound escaped from his mouth.

The images faded and Bethany barely had time to gather her thoughts about what she had just witnessed when another memory started. She found herself in the middle of cheering crowds looking up at a statue of Quinn and herself caught in dramatic poses. She recognised the Stolen City and all the different types of leprechauns applauding: the devious, the mischievous, the friendly, the wise. A group of senior leprechauns were gathered in a semi-circle in front of Quinn. Among them was Hurm Igrig, and going by his worn appearance a large period of time had elapsed since the last memory.

Quinn was the centre of attention and he was turning to greet all the admiring glances he was receiving. An extremely old and important leprechaun draped in masses of jewellery stepped forward, presenting the pooka with a ceremonial purple sash encrusted with a white diamond.

'It has come to the attention of the Leprechaun High Council that you have, with the help of your human colleague, managed to destroy a powerful and dangerous demon that threatened the balance of the physical and spirit realms of Earth.' Pat, Seamus, Donovan and Flannigan waved in recognition at Quinn from the mass of leprechaun faces. 'We congratulate you, Quinn,' the senior leprechaun continued. 'As a mark of respect for your achievements we offer you the position of Honorary Demon Hunter and the key to our city so that you can move freely around our kingdom.'

Quinn bowed as the sash was placed over his head. There was a second burst of applause and cheers, and he waved to the crowd, acknowledging Hurm Igrig, who wore a strained expression as if he was struggling to be polite. As Quinn's gaze passed over the mob of leprechauns he stopped as he reached Gurdo Erlstan. The leprechaun's face looked slightly sunken and he wore a curious smile, a thin, secretive grin that suggested he was not altogether happy at Quinn's success. Something dark stirred in his eyes. He seemed to be focusing on the statue of Quinn and Bethany with surprising intensity.

The crowd let out another cheer and the pooka laughed, but Bethany was sure she detected something strained in that pleasant chortling. The memory faded away as abruptly as the previous one and she pulled the ring from her finger this time. The bedroom appeared around her and Maggie-Maggie looked at her, concerned. 'What is it, dearie? Are you OK?' right-headed Maggie asked.

'Sort of,' Bethany answered. 'There's something odd about this, though. The ring is only showing me specific things.'

'Well, that would make sense if Quinn has charmed it,' left-headed Maggie said. 'He must have wanted to show you something.'

'I know, it's just . . .' Bethany found it difficult to verbalise the sense of disquiet she had. It was something instinctual. She even imagined her own ring was tingling slightly in response, as if warning her.

Right-headed Maggie picked up on her nervousness. 'If something seems wrong with it, you stop it straight away. In fact, maybe you should wait until we have a better idea from your leprechaun friends what is going on.'

'No, it's fine,' Bethany replied sternly. 'I need to find out what he wants to show me.'

She returned the ring to her little finger and found herself back in the Stolen City. Quinn was wandering about a room that bore a passing resemblance to Hurm Igrig's office, although this space was slightly smaller and conspicuously messier. It seemed that Quinn had caused chaos. He had performed some sort of magic on his chair that had caused it to shrink until it was the size of his thumb. Meanwhile, some footage was playing in a sphere of light above his desk, although the ring projecting it must have been damaged in some way as the images were running back and forth repeatedly.

Hurm Igrig stepped into the office and examined the chaotic scene. 'Hmmff . . . Ah, yes, I see you've made the office your own.'

Quinn tittered.

'Well, congratulations on your appointment. It's rare to be given such a prestigious position so quickly.' Beneath the outward show of politeness there was an undercurrent of disapproval that the leprechaun couldn't hide. 'Will your human counterpart be joining you at some point?'

Quinn shook his head.

'A shame. So many stories about her – she sounds rather remarkable. On that subject, it has come to my attention that you have been requesting information on Gurdo Erlstan's investigation into this demon you suspect of surviving. How can I put this . . .' Hurm Igrig cleared his throat and smiled. 'Your position here is largely an honorary one, Quinn. It does the leprechauns good to see a spirit rewarded for their efforts to keep the balance. But please don't feel you have any obligations to pursue investigations, especially investigations that are my responsibility and have been concluded to my satisfaction.'

Quinn looked up. He was busy trying to summon a cup of cloud tea for his guest, but he had clicked his fingers too many times and lots of cups and saucers were appearing across the desk as a result.

Hurm Igrig viewed the mess with disdain. 'I know there were initially interesting reports about a demon that was hiding in mirrors and possessing some lower spirits – a couple of ghosts, an imp, a wood spirit. These sorts of stories often arise after a major demonic event and Gurdo has shown them to be insubstantial reports. Even if these stories were true and if your demon had survived, not only would it be too weak to do anything, it would cause a great deal of concern among the leprechauns that such a demon was on the loose. In short, it would make this department look bad.'

Quinn had cleared most of the cups and saucers off his desk and offered one of the remaining cups of cloud tea to Hurm Igrig. He declined. 'No, thank you. I have to be going. Work commitments. These future crimes always turn up some unexpected surprises.' His bulbous nose twitched and he scratched it distractedly.

A sad, deflated sound issued from Quinn.

As Hurm Igrig made his way out of the door, he paused. 'If you're short of things to do, we need someone to look into a spate of vandalism around the city.'

Quinn looked up hopefully.

'Yes, apparently several statues of yourself and that

human, Bethany Chase, have been damaged by a disgruntled leprechaun.' The elder leprechaun could hardly contain his pleasure at this. 'It's probably a jealous spirit. Nothing to worry about, I'm sure.'

He left Quinn's office a lot more relaxed and content than when he had entered it, Bethany thought.

As the images faded once again Bethany's mind raced. It seemed Hurm Igrig had it in for Quinn as much as he had for Bethany. It did little to lift the knot of anxiety in her belly, though.

The next memory sped towards a street Bethany recognised. Quinn was in front of the statue that she had seen on her first visit to the Stolen City, although the figures were covered in black scorch marks, as if someone had repeatedly slashed at the diamond sculpture in a blind rage. As Quinn arrived there were two leprechauns in blue uniform trying out different spells to remove the magic, without much success.

Quinn moved in as close as he could get and examined the black marks. They were exactly the same scorch marks he had seen on the mirror and he recoiled in shock. He ran back to a waiting elephant-footed chair, a chair being guided by the ghost sisters, Maggie-Maggie.

'You don't look so well, dearie,' right-headed Maggie commented. 'It's not anything bad, is it?' asked her sister quickly.

The pooka gave a strangled sound. He motioned for the ghosts to get the chair moving.

'Do you still want us to take you to the next one?' left-headed Maggie asked him.

He nodded his head vigorously, and the chair moved into action, soon depositing him at the stairs of a wide, domed building decorated in strange symbols. In front of it was a line of statues, and a steady stream of leprechauns passed by, casting admiring glances at the row of sculpted figures. One statue was attracting a lot of attention, though, and as Quinn barged his way through the crowds he could see why. There, standing on a decorative plinth, was another likeness of himself and Bethany disfigured with the black scorch marks. The word *LIARS* had been scrawled across the surface of the statue lots of times, and the sight was causing all sorts of stunned and surprised reactions from the passing leprechauns.

As he reached it, there was a gasp behind him and he turned to find that Maggie-Maggie had followed him. The sisters were horrified at the sight of the damaged statue. 'Who would do such a thing?' right-headed Maggie exclaimed.

Many leprechauns muttered disparagingly at the sisters, commenting that ghosts were not supposed to wander freely about the city. Quinn scanned the crowd, nervously running back and forth, searching for any clue as to a possible culprit.

'She's not in danger, is she?' left-headed Maggie asked in a serious tone.

Quinn did not make any sort of noise.

'I think you need to tell us everything you know,' right-headed Maggie insisted.

But Quinn was examining a crushed object lying by the statue that resembled a crumpled monocle.

The image dissolved. Bethany felt her anxiety building, so real was the sensation that she was immersed in Quinn's life. She struggled to warn him, to turn him away from his path, but it was only a recording, and she was powerless to change a thing. It was almost unbearable when the next memory started and she had to look on, unable to influence the unfolding events.

Quinn was sitting on the back of the elephant chair guided by Maggie-Maggie. They came to a huddle of buildings on the outskirts of the Stolen City and he dismounted, waddled over to the nearest building and moved purposefully along the main hallway. Doorways led off from this corridor, each with a name written above it, alongside a ghostly face of the resident. He wandered down a long line of leprechaun faces. Several occupants greeted him as they left their homes, opening their doors to give him tantalising peeks at their colourful living quarters. It wasn't until he had reached the third floor that he came to the doorway of Gurdo Erlstan, with his long, serious face and his dangling white moustache.

Quinn approached the door and knocked three times. Patiently, he waited. Several residents passed by, smiling in acknowledgment as if they recognised him. He rocked back and forth on his heels and knocked again, and again he waited. When it was clear no one was answering he surveyed the corridor, removed the ceremonial purple sash from his pocket and held the diamond by the door handle. The lock gave a satisfying click and he opened the door and discreetly slipped inside.

The room might have been a pleasant, homely dwelling at one time, resembling a mossy cave with furniture crafted from pieces of reclaimed wood. But someone had destroyed the contents of the room in a fury, overturning tables, chairs, pictures of Gurdo Erlstan's family, bottles of potions, books of protection spells. Everything had been broken and thrown to one side. On the far wall was a collection of mirrors. Beneath the mirrors was a shrine constructed from miniature statues. Bethany felt her stomach tightening in sheer terror as she watched Quinn approach the pile of figurines. She recognised the miniature versions of the statue of herself and Quinn, although all of them had been disfigured and slashed in violent strokes with the black scorch marks. At the foot of this pile was a scaled-down model of the Stolen City, made up of ghostly light and highlighting a single building that Bethany recognised from the court: the leprechauns' bank.

As Quinn was examining this, he was distracted by a glimmer of movement from the mirrors above him and he spun round, expecting someone or something to be standing behind him. There was nothing there, however. A nervous giggle escaped his mouth and he looked up questioningly at the mirrors, scrutinising them more closely. There was a ghost in one, a fire imp in another, a wood spirit in another, and several that each contained different leprechauns. The spirits appeared to be trapped in their separate reflections of the room and they were all waving and gesturing at Quinn with desperate motions. The spirits had faded bodies, as if they had been drained of their energy. A couple of mirrors were empty, obviously awaiting occupants. This vision was disturbing enough, but it was given particular significance when Quinn focused on the prisoner of a small square mirror. Gurdo Erlstan was urgently trying to attract the pooka's attention, writing on the surface of the mirror over and over again: *NOMED NOMED NOMED*. He kept pointing at his face and waving his arms in warning at the doorway.

Bethany realised at the same time as Quinn what the leprechaun was writing. The pooka quickly reached forward to try and free Gurdo, but he could see the door opening in the reflection. He turned and this time there was someone there. A full-sized version of Gurdo Erlstan entered the room, with the same serious, stony face and long moustache. The leprechaun appeared shocked at Quinn's presence in his room and took a step back as if he was about to raise the alarm. Something shifted in his face, though. He scanned the room and mirrors, realising that Quinn knew what was going on. A smile spread across Gurdo's face, but it was not a smile that belonged to that leprechaun, it was a nasty, malicious sneer. It was the mocking grin of a demon and it broke through the imitation of Gurdo Erlstan.

'I've learned a few new tricks since we last met, Quinn,' the leprechaun imposter said, although the voice rasped with a sinister, disturbing sound. Bethany recognised that voice immediately; it was the mocking voice of the Jackomuss demon that had tried to kill her at the heart of the Spellbound Hotel. It strode in front of the mirrors, casting an admiring glance at its own work. 'Impressive magic, don't you think? Not only do I steal their appearance, I steal their very spirit. Gurdo has been particularly helpful. He's a very clever and methodical leprechaun, which has helped me plan something quite special for you, Quinn.'

Quinn reacted instantly as the demon attacked. The pooka defended himself against a crackling beam of energy that shot from the demon's fingertips. It rebounded off him as he performed a defensive spell, but he wasn't prepared for the speed of the next attack and he was thrown on to his back amid an eruption of blue sparks. The leprechaun stood over him, throwing up his arms. The image of Gurdo Erlstan wavered uncertainly before being replaced by the flickering of a large black flame. The blackness leaped into the air above Quinn, spreading itself like a flung net. Darkness fell over him and the room vanished.

Bethany might have screamed, or it might have been Quinn's strangled shrieking as he tried to struggle free. He became entangled in the blackness and tore at it as if tearing at a sheet. In the confusion, a hand grabbed at his own, then another hand. Something wrestled with him in the dark, clutching and struggling. Inadvertently, he pulled his opponent towards him and found himself staring at his own features. The doppelganger grinned with his grin, laughed with his laugh. Quinn tried to pull himself free from its grip but it mirrored each movement he made. The two rolled across the floor, breaking free from the darkness and fighting in the clutter of the room.

With one almighty heave, Quinn managed to wrench himself from the demon's hold and fell back against a wall. He turned to open the door but the door refused to budge. He swivelled his head and noticed, too late, that the room and everything in it was back to front. The demon, having assumed Quinn's form, quickly retreated through the glistening surface of one wall. That wall looked out on to the real room. With a shudder, Quinn realised that he was trapped in a reflection of Gurdo Erlstan's room, that he was inside one of the vacant mirrors he had seen. He ran after the demon but was too slow. An arm wrestled with his own, pulling the ring free from his hand before disappearing through the surface of the mirror.

The demon pulled itself upright. It fixed the ring on its finger and examined the oval mirror containing the miniature form of Quinn struggling to escape. The demon spoke in its nasty, sneering tone, a sound like cracking ice. 'I am going to have such fun with you, Quinn,' it said, examining its new body as if it was appreciating a piece of fine tailoring. 'I'm going to do quite terrible things in your name. Believe me, they won't be worshipping you as a hero once I've finished with you, oh no. And your little friend . . .' It picked up one of the scarred statues of Bethany and Quinn and laughed in the pooka's characteristic gurgling, hiccupping laugh. 'I have something special planned for her, too. She's going to watch you do all sorts of terrible things, and she won't know what to believe or who to trust. Maybe I'll leave little clues like I did with you. Just so she knows, when it is too late, that it was me all along, getting my revenge.' The demon grinned its sickening grin. It stroked the arrangement of pink gems on the ring and laughed. 'That'll be fun, won't it, Bethany?'

With a shriek, Bethany wrenched the ring from her finger and hurled it away from her. Her blood ran cold and she trembled with the shock. She fell against the door of her bedroom and Maggie-Maggie rushed towards her. Alarmed, the ghost sisters tried to help her up, but their arms passed uselessly through Bethany's physical body. 'What is it, dearie? What's wrong?'

Bethany could hardly breathe. 'It's Quinn. The demon has Quinn!'

CHAPTER FOURTEEN

THE FULL QUINN MAKEOVER

By the next morning a sizeable crowd had gathered outside Aunt Bess's house. Reporters crammed the doorway to try and get interviews and photographers pushed up against the windows in the hope of capturing a photo of the winning family. Mr and Mrs Chase had spent over an hour in the bathroom applying the various Quinn products, then nervously re-applying them. Aunt Bess was doing her best to calm her animals, but she looked as agitated as her pets.

Maggie-Maggie had spent most of her time attempting to get the ring to give up its secrets for her but, try as she might, it did not play the recordings again, and she concluded that it had been enchanted so that it could only be seen by Bethany.

This made Bethany feel even worse. The demon had been manipulating her all this time. It wasn't Hurm Igrig at all. She felt foolish and upset that she hadn't seen through the deception sooner. Even the ring was meant as a cruel reminder that she had been tricked by the demon and there was little she could do to stop it. It would do no good going to the leprechauns now to alert them about what was happening, unless they could find some way of making the ring replay its memories, and that looked doubtful. The demon had covered its tracks and was toying with Bethany.

'I'll go,' she told the sisters.

'But the demon!' left-headed Maggie exclaimed. 'It's too dangerous,' agreed her sister.

'I wanted to get close to it. This is my chance,' Bethany said firmly. 'There was something Flannigan said about mirror magic, used to impersonate other spirits. The demon would have to keep those spirits trapped and nearby to drain their energy. That means if I can get near to the demon I can get near Quinn. If I can break the magic it's using on him, we might have a chance at stopping the demon.'

The sisters seemed unconvinced. 'We could wait for Flannigan to come back?' right-headed Maggie suggested. 'Let him know what's happening.'

'There's not enough time. We can't back down now.'

'Well . . .' The sisters shared an anxious glance. 'We'll come with you. You can't do this alone.'

'I know. We need to be careful, though. My parents will be there and I don't want them hurt. They're already suffering enough from his cursed products. But they might help create a distraction. You can do that too. We need to find the mirror containing Quinn and break it. You can help search for it —' Bethany stopped short as her mother's head peered round her bedroom door.

'Come on, Bethany. Aren't you ready yet?' Mrs Chase's voice trembled with excitement. A cloud of black and gold hung over her face in the spirit realm but Mrs Chase was blissfully unaware. She was heavily made up and Bethany felt sick knowing that the Quinn products were cursed by the demon. She dreaded to think what effect it was really having as it drained her mother's spirit. 'Who are you talking to, anyway?'

'Oh . . . um, no one, just getting ready,' Bethany replied as casually as she could.

'Well, get a move on. There's TV cameras and everything! The limousine will be here almost any minute.' Mrs Chase ran downstairs.

Bethany was pulling on her shoes when there was another knock at the door. Aunt Bess appeared. She wore an expression of deep concern.

'Bethany, I just wanted to say . . .' She struggled to find the words and held her hands nervously. 'What I said yesterday, about sometimes having a funny feeling about things, well . . . I have that feeling now. I don't think you should go. It feels wrong. *Dangerous*.' She sighed. 'There, I've said it.'

Bethany was taken aback. She didn't know how to reply.

Aunt Bess continued, 'I know I can't change your parents' mind, but you still have a choice. You can stay here. I could tell them that you're not feeling well.'

'I . . .' Bethany wanted to explain to her aunt. She wanted to tell her exactly why she had to go, even though she knew it was dangerous.

As if on cue the doorbell rang and Mrs Chase issued a series of high-pitched squeals. 'This is it! This is it! Come on.'

'Look, I need to go,' Bethany told her aunt sincerely. 'I can't explain it but . . . I have to do this. Trust me.'

Aunt Bess chewed her lip. 'If you're sure it feels right, Bethany.'

She nodded.

'Well, then . . .' her aunt murmured, clearly disappointed that she had not talked Bethany out of it. The worried frown deepened on her forehead. 'Please be careful,' she said quietly. The doorbell rang again and the cats and dogs erupted with noise. Aunt Bess hurried downstairs to herd her pets away from all the commotion.

Bethany felt the twisting lump of nerves in her stomach tighten. She turned round to Maggie-Maggie for some reassurance, but the ghost sisters had completely vanished. Her mother reappeared, clutched Bethany's arm and dragged her down to the front door, where Mr Chase was waiting, equally frenzied with excitement. He sounded breathless and panicky. 'Are you ready? How do I look? I think this is it. Just act casual in front of the cameras. Just be yourself.' This would have been more useful advice if he didn't look so Quinn-like.

There was a series of bright flashes from the assembled photographers as Mr Chase flung the door open. A man wearing a chauffeur's outfit (but otherwise looking exactly like Quinn) stood at the entrance and ushered Bethany and her parents out of the house. They followed him to a long, sleek limousine, moving through a gauntlet of journalists shouting questions, photographers aiming cameras, and cheering fans waving banners. Mr and Mrs Chase stopped to smile with their wide, bright grins at the crowds, whereas Bethany could hardly look at them. Viewed through her glasses she could see they were covered in the tiny golden hooks, draining their energy slowly to the spirit realm. Bethany grew cold, realising where those streams of light were leading.

As the chauffeur held open the door of the limousine for her she caught a glimpse of something else peculiar. She could see Maggie-Maggie was sneaking into the back of the vehicle. The sisters were pulling their ghost bodies through the back of the car to hide themselves in the boot. This went completely unnoticed and Bethany was forced into her seat as her mother entered the car, eager to get going.

'I can't believe it's actually happening,' Mrs Chase sighed.

'Mum, have you wondered why it is that you're so obsessed by Quinn when you didn't even know who he was not so long ago?' Bethany asked, beginning to find her mother's condition exasperating.

'Quinn's affected us all,' Mrs Chase replied.

Mr Chase nodded. 'He's changed our lives.'

That was true. But not in a good way. Bethany could see the effects the demon was having as she peered out the window of the moving car, and it did little to settle the fear rising in her. The passing streets were full of people who she could see were all being drained of their energy. The car journey followed the trickles of light that were drawing towards a point in the distance. It was where the demon was waiting. And judging by the power he had over the city, he would be stronger now than she had ever witnessed him.

Something caught her eye outside the window. For a brief moment, she thought she had glimpsed a ginger cat scampering in the same direction as the limousine. Groups of Quinn fans cheered as the vehicle passed them by, Mr and Mrs Chase leaning out of the windows to wave at them. Bethany thought she saw another cat running along the pavement, this one a dark brown, but it disappeared among a crowd of pedestrians. She longed to see the black cat with orange eyes so that she could tell Hurm Igrig what was happening.

There was no one to help her, though, as the limousine glided through an expensive-looking area of London. A series of tall, grandiose houses passed by on either side, each more magnificent than the last. Ahead, there was a waiting crowd. The people were gathered by a street that had been closed off at either end, with security guards in Quinn get-up patrolling the wide electric gates.

'A private street,' Mr Chase commented in an impressed tone. 'Very exclusive. Which house does Quinn live in?'

'Which house?' The chauffeur pulled up by the gates and flashed a pass at the tight line of security guards. Quinn fans were screaming and chanting his name in a wave of hysteria. 'He owns the whole street,' the driver remarked.

While Mr and Mrs Chase stared at the row of houses in awe, Bethany looked in horror at the sight in front of her. The streams of light were congregating at one house, a particularly smart dwelling positioned in the middle of the street. The light was draining to a single, dark point hidden inside the centre of the building. The tears in the spirit realm were the worst here, and she could feel an unpleasant, heavy effect on her spirit as if she was being dragged forwards. She glanced briefly at her parents and the driver, amazed that they could sense nothing unusual.

The limousine glided to a halt. The driver opened the back door and helped his passengers out, directing them to a red carpet that led up a set of steps towards a front door. Bethany's parents raced forward but as the driver ushered her out of the car, his head briefly passed through a patch of the torn spirit realm. He looked over at the ghost sisters clambering out of the boot of his car and his face filled with horror. 'Ghosts!' he muttered. He tripped backwards in shock, out of the rip in the spirit realm, and hesitated, no longer able to see them. He composed himself. 'Sorry, I thought I could see . . .' His voice trailed off, and Bethany and the sisters moved quickly up the steps.

'He could see you,' Bethany whispered. 'He could see you through that tear.'

'We know,' the sisters said together, flustered.

Tentatively, they approached the stone steps leading up to the house, wondering what other surprises lay in store for them. At the bottom step they could just make out a thin semi-transparent barrier like the one Bethany had seen in the Stolen City. It wrapped round the entire house in a wide cone. The sisters looked at Bethany in alarm. Their ghost bodies pushed against the glowing surface but were repelled. Desperately, they tried a second time to pass through the barrier, but were knocked backwards again. 'He must have it protected,' right-headed Maggie said, aghast.

Bethany moved through it easily as she stepped forwards. 'It seems OK for me.'

'The demon knows you're coming, dearie. He's probably put this up to stop any spirits getting close to him that he doesn't want near. I dare say the leprechauns have been trying to get close.'

'Bethany, what are you doing just standing there?' her father asked, having bounded up the steps and now waiting at the front door for her.

She turned briefly to the ghost sisters and spoke under her breath. 'I can't let my parents go in there on their own. I need to do this. If I'm not back soon find Flannigan and tell him what has happened.'

'But it's a trap, Bethany. Don't you see? This is what the demon wants.'

'I can't do anything by running away,' Bethany said forcefully. She ran to join her parents as the front door swung open. Together, they stepped inside.

'Oh my!' Mr Chase uttered.

'It's gorgeous,' Mrs Chase sighed.

The three of them stood at the edge of a wide, luxurious lobby fashioned from pure white marble. Elegant columns and arches stretched in front of them. A selection of statues, vases and works of art were interspersed among the alcoves. Bethany recognised famous paintings of kings, popes, beautiful models and landscapes, yet all had been reworked to include Quinn's grinning face.

'I think that's part of the Parthenon,' Mr Chase remarked in amazement at a classical statue that had had a wide grin chiselled on to it.

'It's so tasteful,' Mrs Chase gushed.

Bethany rushed through the lobby, quickly making her way to a set of spiral staircases and climbing them urgently. She needed to find Quinn. 'We don't have time.'

'You seem keen all of a sudden,' Mr Chase said.

Bethany reached the top of the staircase and nearly bumped into a figure waiting there. Her first impression was that she had collided with Quinn the demon, but as soon as she inspected the head staring at her with a curiously dazed expression, she realised that it was a person wearing an extremely realistic Quinn mask. The person waited patiently for Mr and Mrs Chase to arrive, then turned away and strode down a long corridor. There was a set of pink and yellow striped doors, guarded by another two people wearing the same Quinn masks, and they stepped aside to let the visitors through.

Inside, a vast workshop stretched before them. There were lots of tables and benches occupying the space, each full of Quinn products. Masked Quinn clones were working silently at the desks, measuring, testing and packaging the products. Their eyes were strangely lifeless and Bethany wondered what effects the masks were having on them, and what could have possessed them to wear them in the first place. At the far end, a separate office looked out on to the workshop. In it, there was a large swivel chair, turned away from them, with a tiny tuft of pink hair peeking over the top of it. What only Bethany, with her glasses, could see, was that this figure was the focal point for all the streaming currents of light and it was drinking them greedily, feeding itself on the spirit energy.

Mr and Mrs Chase cooed and gasped with interest as they were led past benches full of new products. Bethany was trying to fight her own rising panic. The closer she got to the demon, the more she could feel its power pulling on the spirit realm. When they reached the office, she felt an overwhelming sensation of hopelessness, as if her spirit was being drained too. The ring on her finger tingled in alarm as if warning her to run.

The chair swivelled round and the immense, plump form of Quinn greeted them, although now Bethany could see how wrong she had been to assume that this was Quinn in the first place. The mimicry was exact apart from one crucial detail. The eyes flickered with malevolent glee. They fell on Bethany now, acknowledging everything that she knew, confirming her worst fears.

'Quinn, it's actually you!' screeched Mrs Chase.

Mr Chase made a meek, bowing gesture. 'Sir, it's *such* an honour. You've affected us all.'

Mrs Chase curtsied. 'You've changed our lives.'

'Stay away from him!' Bethany blurted out as her father moved forward to shake the demon's hand. 'That's not Quinn. It's a demon.'

Nobody moved.

'*Bethany!*' Mrs Chase scolded her. She tittered in a nervous tone.

Mr Chase added, 'Sorry, our daughter has a rather unusual sense of humour.'

Quinn towered over them and teased out a tense, uncomfortable silence for as long as possible. Eventually, he spoke. His voice had an unmistakably cruel tone to it and had a rasping, otherworldly quality that made Bethany's parents gawp in surprise. 'Your daughter is right. I am a demon and I am extremely dangerous,' he stated.

Mr and Mrs Chase were unsure how to react. They stared at each other, dumbfounded. For a moment, Bethany thought they had come to their senses, but they burst into fits of laughter, thinking that this was some preposterous joke. The demon joined in, giggling and cackling in its own mocking tone.

'Isn't he funny?' Mrs Chase said to her husband.

'A demon, indeed,' Mr Chase exclaimed merrily. 'That really is marvellous.'

Bethany was silent. Her attention had shifted to the office wall that the demon had been facing. It was covered with the spirit mirrors that she had seen in the recording, and there, at the very centre, was the oval mirror containing the desperate figure of Quinn. His tiny form was slumped to one side, so faded and weak that he couldn't even lift his head to look at Bethany. She felt a wave of despair. She had been counting on him to help fight the demon, but he looked utterly devastated. Then Bethany noticed another captive, a row across. Donovan stared out at her from one of the mirrors, terrified, signalling at her to run. Instinctively, she took a step towards her friends to help them. The demon blocked her way.

'I have a little something for you,' he muttered darkly. He gave a wide, gleaming grin, then gestured at the nearby table loaded with Quinn products. In the centre of the table were several masks laid out in a row, looking like severed heads, each one grinning idiotically. 'A new product for you to try on,' he told Bethany's parents.

Mr and Mrs Chase needed little persuasion and leaped forward.

'NO!' Bethany screamed, trying to block their way. She could see that the masks were laced deeply with the leprechaun gold, stronger than any of the other cursed Quinn products. 'Mum, Dad, you have to listen to me, he's using magic on you. They're evil, don't touch them.'

'It's just a bit of fun, Bethany,' her mother reassured her as she barged past.

'No, it's not. You don't understand!' But it was no good. Bethany could see that the lure of the magic was too strong for her parents to resist after such exposure. They rushed to pull the masks on, although the masks seemed to move and slither as they handled them, sucking on to their heads with an unpleasant schlepping noise.

'That's a snug fit,' Mrs Chase commented.

Mr Chase murmured in agreement. 'What do they do exactly?' he asked.

They were unrecognisable. The surface of the masks seemed to come alive, mimicking the demon Quinn's face as perfect clones.

The demon giggled malevolently, quietly at first, then building in force until he roared with hysterical laughter. 'They do whatever I want them to,' he said viciously. He clicked his fingers. 'To attention.'

Mr and Mrs Chase snapped to attention like guards on duty. They both laughed nervously. 'This is peculiar,' Mrs Chase said. 'How does it —?'

'Silence,' the demon commanded. Both of Bethany's parents fell silent. The demon chuckled to himself. 'Isn't that better?' he asked, then, realising they could not respond, he added, 'Nod.'

Mr and Mrs Chase nodded.

A shriek of anger burst out of Bethany and she charged

at the demon, catching him with several blows to his chest. A crackle of blue energy erupted from his fingertips. It connected with Bethany's body, deflecting off the protection spell Flannigan had given her. The force of it flung her backwards, sprawling to the ground. She thought she could hear her parents crying her name and moving to help her but the demon jerked them back into place.

'You see,' the demon said, addressing her parents, 'your daughter is right. I am a demon. That's why Bethany came looking for me. I knew she would. She made the very foolish mistake of trying to destroy me once before, and she thinks she can finish the job this time around. Correct, Bethany?'

She glowered at the demon, refusing to answer.

'Yes, you had nearly wiped me out completely.' The demon mused over the memory. 'I know you saw me escape after the hotel collapsed. It took me a long time to gain my power once again. I had to feed off lesser ghosts and pathetically weak spirits just to get my strength back. It was difficult at first. I had known such fabulous power, I was on the verge of becoming as mighty as a god, and suddenly all that was lost . . . because of *you*.' His voice mangled the word. 'Because of *you* I had to feed on scraps. The shame would have destroyed me if I had not taken one last piece of magic with me, one last trick.' He tapped one of the mirrors. 'And that was how I began my rise once more.'

He examined the spirit mirrors carefully. Each reflection of the office was like a tiny cell, containing the captive spirits. Gurdo Erlstan was there in his square mirror, and there were also several terrified ghosts, a fire spirit that had dimmed considerably and, of course, Quinn and Donovan. She had never seen the pooka looking so weak before.

'Quite an impressive collection, isn't it?' the demon said boastfully. 'They were all very useful to me. But when Gurdo came looking for me – oh, it was such perfection – it changed everything. I had no idea of the riches that waited for me in the Stolen City. And to top it all, I could get close to Quinn. I could plan the most perfect revenge.'

Bethany picked herself up. She glanced briefly at Quinn and her parents. 'I saw what you did to him. I got your little message.'

'Ah yes, the ring. I was proud of that little touch. I wondered how long it would take you to realise the answers were right under your nose.' The demon sighed, savouring the moment. 'Quinn was rather hopeless. He fell into my trap so easily. And I've heard things haven't gone so well for you.' He gestured at the collection of captive spirits and, in particular, the dishevelled figure of Donovan.

Bethany tried not to react at the sight of the terrified leprechaun, even though it made her sense of hopelessness grow.

'I caught him snooping around last night, trying to find a way in. He's been most cooperative. He told me all about your latest adventures, your trial and how his little friends helped you escape the leprechaun prison. I'm amazed at the loyalty you command from your friends but their sacrifice will have been quite useless. If anything, they've helped my plan ahead of schedule. I wanted to make sure the leprechauns turned against you and Quinn, that you would no longer enjoy the hero status given to you in the Stolen City. It seems I've succeeded. Once I'm finished here, you'll become criminals of the worst kind. When they find you and put you on trial a second time it won't end in a lenient prison sentence, it will end in soul removal and your friends won't be able to save you from that. It is the most agonising, unbearable punishment possible.' He paused to savour the thought. 'A perfect revenge, I feel.'

Bethany had manoeuvred herself in front of the table containing the Quinn masks. Carefully, she put her arm behind her back and tried to feel for anything solid. She needed to keep the demon distracted. 'What do you mean, when they find us?'

'I'm sure it hasn't escaped your notice what my magic has done in the spirit realm. I have upset the precious balance the leprechauns are so keen to protect. When the walls of reality come crashing down – and they will come crashing down – the leprechauns will come running in force to try and repair the damage. It won't be me they find, though. It will be you and Quinn.' His voice and appearance shifted suddenly, morphing into Donovan's features. 'And while that's keeping them busy I'll be on my way to the Stolen City to get some more of their gold, so I will,' he said in the leprechaun's friendly accent. 'With enough of that gold I'll be as powerful as a god, I'll be stronger than I ever was. And that will just be the beginning of my rise. The leprechauns have access to other worlds, worlds I fully intend to explore and conquer.'

Out of the corner of her eye, Bethany saw that some light returned to Quinn's spirit body just as the demon stopped mimicking him. It was as if the demon had to be actively impersonating Quinn to drain his energy. Her hand fell on a solid metal canister and she seized the moment. In two bounding steps she lunged at the demon and smashed the canister over his head, connecting with his forehead in a loud crack. He screeched in fury. For a moment his body fluttered – briefly it was Donovan, briefly it was Quinn, and for a moment it was a monstrous black flame, but of such a size that Bethany gazed at it in horrified fascination. It was like a blazing furnace of blackness turning in on itself, drinking in the steady stream of light from the spirit realm.

Bethany tried to reach for the mirror containing the real Quinn, but she was distracted for a split second as she noticed her parents suddenly trying to free themselves from their masks, along with all the other clones in the workshop. Had the demon's control momentarily slipped?

'Mum? Dad?'

'Bethany!' she heard them both call out.

They were silenced quickly, though, as the demon regained his power. The leering face of Quinn barked out, 'Stop!' All the struggling clones froze.

Bethany made one last effort to snatch at the mirror containing Quinn, in the hope of smashing it, but saw that she was too late. The demon aimed a crackling bolt of energy at her and this one caught her directly in the back, causing a searing flood of pain, followed by a sudden wrenching sensation. She felt her spirit being thrown from her physical body, diminishing in size until she was no bigger than a leprechaun. She spun in freefall, then felt herself plunge through a shimmering layer and land on the floor of the room from which she had just been ejected. Confused, she gazed at her surroundings and saw that everything was back to front.

The real Quinn gurgled sadly and tried to help her up. He was having some difficulty as the feeble light that made up his body wavered. He stumbled back. With a sinking feeling she realised she had been trapped in the mirror with him, and she peered up at the transparent layer that faced out on to the real room as the demon approached. Its demented expression surveyed them, gigantic and gloating. 'That was your great effort to destroy me, was it? Such a disappointment, Bethany.'

'You can't do this!' Bethany shouted futilely. She banged at the surface of the mirror.

'I already have,' he hissed. 'I need you two to stay together. I have to make sure the leprechauns find you when this whole reality rips apart. You can watch over Quinn in the meantime. He really doesn't look well, does he? And I'm still not quite finished using his powers of mischief.' He examined the huge cracks and almighty tears spreading in the spirit realm. 'Although it won't be long now.'

The demon returned to his chair and swung it round to scrutinise his workshop. The clones were still caught in their various positions of struggle. 'Back to work!' he commanded them, and immediately the workforce resumed their quiet, compliant jobs.

'And you two,' the demon said, gesturing at Bethany's parents. 'Put that on the table.'

Bethany looked on in vain. Her parents were lifting her physical body and placing it on to the nearby table, before taking their places at either side of the demon. In a mechanical motion they turned their backs on her, and it was impossible to tell if they were even aware of what had happened to themselves or their daughter.

CHAPTER FIFTEEN

A SUITABLE DISTRACTION

'What have I done? *What have I done?*'

Bethany slumped to the floor, hanging her head. Quinn lay in front of her, too frail to even sit up. Bethany was pained to see him this way.

'What are we going to do? We need to escape. We need to stop him.' She spoke to the pooka but really she was speaking to herself, trying to focus her thoughts.

Quinn gave her a weak smile, but she could tell he was too sick to act.

Bethany hid the worried expression on her face, knowing that it would only make his condition worse. She stood up, pacing back and forth, struggling to throw off her sense of hopelessness. 'He's feeding on your spirit,' she said. 'There must be some way to stop him, we can't just sit here and do nothing. We need to fight.'

The pooka nodded slowly in agreement.

'If you just had enough strength we could maybe find some way of breaking out of this mirror – it's how the demon is draining you. Then we might at least have a hope of stopping his power over everyone.' She crouched down by him. 'Do you have any energy left? Any magic that you could use?'

Quinn considered the request seriously for several moments. With a determined air, he sat himself upright and tried to stand up. Intense concentration filled his face. His faint body gained definition and he took several faltering steps forward to the surface of the mirror. He raised a hand purposefully but the effort caused his whole body to flicker and fade. He winced in pain and collapsed to the floor.

'No, stop!' Bethany said in a desperate tone. 'You're too weak. Stop.'

Reluctantly, he dropped back to his lying position.

'It's OK,' Bethany reassured him, patting his arm. 'I'll think of something.'

Quinn seemed comforted by this. In truth, there was nothing Bethany could do. She realised that. She had no magic to use. Her protection spell had been exhausted, and, by the look of it, her luck had completely run out. All she could do was wait. She dared not imagine what would happen when the boundary between the spirit realm and the physical realm was torn apart. Would people be able to see spirits and ghosts and demons? Would they go out of their minds, as large numbers seemed to have done under the influence of the Quinn products?

She trembled. She fell against the wall, her spirit body feeling heavy and weak. Distractedly, she scratched her tingling hand. 'I should have known,' she muttered to herself. 'I should have seen it. Hurm Igrig wasn't the demon.' She felt angry at herself and frustrated at her own stupidity. *Why had she not realised sooner? It wasn't the cat that was cursing her, it was the demon Quinn.* 'I got it so wrong,' Bethany said to Quinn, trying to explain why she had let him down. 'I'm sorry.'

Quinn gurgled sadly, making the sort of noise that suggested he, too, had got it all wrong. He squeezed her hand, but the gesture caused a sharp, intense streak of pain from Bethany's fingers.

'Ow!' The ring that Flannigan had given her stung her as if it was burning. It must have been reacting to the sustained curse that she was now under. Bethany pulled it free from her finger and threw it away from her. 'Not much use to me now,' she sighed.

Quinn lifted his head questioningly.

'Not you,' Bethany told him. She glanced at the ring. It was rolling on the ground where it had landed. At first, it seemed to be spinning as though it hadn't fully come to rest, but as she watched it, it began moving faster. It spun round lots of times in a blur until it stopped suddenly like a disrupted compass finding magnetic north. The ring pointed at Quinn and rolled towards him, slowly at first, then quick and certain. It collided with his hand and he stirred, squinting down at the object. Something bright came alight in his face and he clutched at the jewelled ring, blinking disbelievingly at it.

For the first time, Quinn spluttered with the hint of genuine, warm laughter. The green jewel flashed excitedly in response.

'What is it?' Bethany asked, her interest perking up.

The pooka didn't have time to tell her. Swiftly, he slid the ring on to his thumb and it flashed with a brilliant white light. Bethany remembered Maggie-Maggie's warning about never placing the ring on your right thumb and she took a step back. A single white flame flared from the band of gold. It flickered and danced, then spread like a catching fire, moving up and across Quinn's hand. Quinn was smiling, and as the white flames engulfed his body his pale spirit surged with light.

'Quinn, what *is that*?' she exclaimed, even as she remembered the peculiar effect of the white flame that she had handled in court. She could see that it was revitalising Quinn's body. The energy seemed to be returning to him, at first in a trickle, then a steady stream, then a flood. This provoked a reaction outside the mirror. They both turned to see the demon surveying his workshop, clutching at his head apparently suffering a sudden, inexplicable pain.

'Whatever you're doing, do it quickly,' Bethany warned him.

Quinn rushed at the surface of the mirror and pushed his hands against the transparent pane. It quivered and rippled in response to the white flames, separating like a draining liquid. He gurgled with laughter and reached his hand out for Bethany to join him, and no sooner had she clutched a hold than they were tumbling out of the hole in the mirror, falling down to the floor far, far below.

Spirit bodies have no bones to break, Bethany told herself as she shrieked, colliding with the solid substance of the floor. As she landed beside Quinn, their spirits hit the ground and submerged into it as if they had landed in particularly soft mud. It was a strange experience, not altogether pleasant, and she peeled her spirit body free. They examined each other. Out here, they were no bigger than rodents.

'Can't you make us bigger?' Bethany asked.

They both glanced up, though, as the demon came charging towards the mirrors. The pooka grabbed her hand and dragged her underneath the legs of the nearby table. His entire body was blazing with the white flames. Bethany could feel that it was, in almost every way, the direct opposite to the black flames of the demon. She felt a sense of hope again, of renewed energy.

'WHAT HAVE YOU DONE?' the demon screeched as he found the empty mirror. He raged with fury, the fury so great that his mimicry of Quinn flickered uncertainly, briefly revealing the black furnace of flames, although diminished in power. 'HOW DARE YOU INTERFERE! HOW DARE YOU TURN MY MAGIC BACK ON ME!'

Bethany and Quinn scurried towards the edge of the table, moving as quickly as they could to get to the door. A bolt of crackling blue flashed past them and sent the table above them crashing against the wall. A cascade of Quinn products fell about them, scattering across the floor. Bethany shrieked as several giant masks fell in front of her, grinning diabolically. The real Quinn slapped a hand over her mouth. He winked, then clicked his fingers. The white flames surrounding him surged brightly and the two of them slipped through the solid substance of the floor just as another burst of magical energy exploded above them.

This time, they glided gently to the ground, as Quinn used some of his flourishing magic. They came to rest in among the white marble columns of the lobby.

'You've got your magic back,' Bethany said in amazement.

He chuckled mischievously and held up the ring on his thumb.

'Well, we have to get outside. Then we might be able to get some help. I'll create a distraction, OK?' Bethany said.

Quinn nodded.

They turned together, sensing the thundering approach of the demon as he hurtled down the stairs, his clone workers just behind him. Bethany tried to get a glimpse of her parents in the group but had to duck out of the way as another spray of the blue magic ricocheted off a nearby column, hitting an ornate Ming vase that shattered into hundreds of pieces with the impact.

'Run!' Bethany shouted. Quinn sprinted towards the doorway at the front of the building whilst Bethany ran directly across the demon's line of vision, waving her arms and causing another series of magical blows to be unleashed around her. A painting of a pope reworked with Quinn's grinning head turned instantly to a blackened, scorched crisp as the magic hit it. A medieval tapestry burst into flames.

Terrified, Bethany darted behind a column and looked around her. The demon's magic must have been weakened by the effort of his attacks as all the clones in the lobby were moving sluggishly as if dazed, some pulling at their masks. She glanced over at the front door and could make out her parents swaying back and forth in a stupor. Instinctively, she took a step towards them. She caught sight of Quinn nearby, heading to the front door, but as Bethany turned back, a dark shape towered over her. The demon had effortlessly appeared beside her and she stumbled backwards, with nowhere to run, exposed and helpless.

A taunting, demented cackle issued from the demon's sneering mouth. He was trying to maintain Quinn's form but his entire body was warping and flickering as his magic failed. He aimed a flood of sparks from his fingertips at the tiny figure of the real Quinn darting towards the entrance of the house. The hit was direct and Quinn skidded across the marble floor with the full impact of the blast. His spirit hit the door with such force that he passed through it instantly.

The demon raged at this, rushing after the pooka,

barging past Bethany's parents and nearly ripping the front door off its hinges. Quickly, Bethany followed. An unusual sight greeted her as she made it to the entrance. There, in the street below them, was a seething mass of cats. Hundreds of them had gathered in front of the house, collected in front of the barrier at the bottom of the steps that had repelled Maggie-Maggie. Ginger cats, fat tabbies, albinos, wild tomcats, scrawny strays, finely groomed pedigree cats; all were patiently grouped together behind a single black cat with eerie orange eyes and all were staring up at the demon. The ghost sisters stood behind the mass of animals.

'Hurm Igrig!' Bethany shouted. 'Maggie-Maggie!'

The demon froze. He took in the bizarre sight of the cats and noticed all the attention it was generating with the crowds at the end of the street. The demon was struggling to keep hold of Quinn's appearance, his face blackening and his good-natured smile looking more like an unpleasant snarl. He tried to imitate the pooka's characteristic laugh, but that laugh stalled as soon as he saw the real Quinn pick himself up and run the last few paces towards the spirit barrier. All at once the demon realised what Quinn was trying to do. It lifted its arm to hurl one last bolt of magical energy at him, but a figure barged into him. Mr Chase had stumbled forward blindly as he tried to rip the mask from his head and inadvertently elbowed the demon out of the way.

It was just enough time for Quinn to make it to the barrier and push through it as he had the cursed mirror. The white flame flared as it burned a hole in the barrier. The waiting cats flooded through the space, led by Hurm Igrig, and Bethany thought she could hear faint voices calling out to one another, voices that she recognised.

'Secure the perimeter,' Hurm Igrig commanded.

'Target in view,' Flannigan announced. 'Close in.'

'Retrieval team approaching,' Seamus said.

The cats swarmed up the stairs. They moved together like a single, fluid creature. The demon screamed, partly in anger, partly in fear, and retreated from the advancing tide of felines. 'Stop them!' he commanded Bethany's parents, and they snapped to attention like two puppets jerked upwards on strings. As the demon fled through the lobby, Mr and Mrs Chase tried to close the door on the approaching cats. A ginger tom with a white face slipped past them and sneezed at them three times, very precisely, and Bethany's parents fell to the floor, unconscious. It peered over at Bethany.

'Come on!' she heard Flannigan call out to her. 'Get on my back, you deserve to see this.'

'Flannigan, what are you doing?' Bethany asked urgently as she clambered on top of the ginger cat.

'You'll see.'

The feline raced ahead to join a group of cats running in formation behind Hurm Igrig. She could hear them calling out to her as they all bounded up the steps. 'Excellent work.'

'It's a real honour.'

'Outstanding job.'

The last voice was Pat's. 'We always knew you had it in you, girl.'

'But . . .' Bethany hardly knew what they meant and it certainly wasn't the time to ask questions. The demon stood in front of them, having decided to try and fend off the cats with magic. It was firing off sparking bolts, but the demon's energy was dwindling and the blows were rebounding off the cats. In minutes they had surrounded him in a tight circle and the demon spun round. He became increasingly desperate and tried to attack them physically, lashing out with his fists and trying to stamp on them with his feet. There were too many, though. They leaped on his back, they coiled around his legs, they clawed at his arms. So many rushed him at once that he was quickly covered in them, cocooned in a tower of cat fur and claw.

The black cat with the orange eyes surveyed this with a steady gaze. 'Now,' commanded Hurm Igrig.

At once, the mass of cats dropped to the floor. The body that had been there moments before disintegrated. In its place was the demon in its true form: a black flame, reduced to a single flickering tongue of darkness snapping at the air.

The cat with the orange eyes twitched its nose. Its body shrank down, morphing into the familiar lumpy form of Hurm Igrig. He dusted himself down and strolled forward. 'I think we're safe to dissolve our cloaking forms now,' he muttered discreetly.

The cat bodies shifted and warped, fur disappearing, limbs re-shaping, until the familiar features of the leprechauns appeared in place of the felines. Some of the leprechauns stepped forward to maintain the circle around the demon, holding up a hand with a ring shining with the white flame.

Hurm Igrig cleared his throat. 'Demon, you have broken numerous leprechaun laws. You have stolen leprechaun gold, impersonated spirits, used widespread curses to gain power, and upset the very balance that sustains the reality of the spirit and physical realms. The ultimate punishment for these crimes is soul removal, and I fully expect the leprechaun court to find you guilty on all counts.' His sombre face surveyed the demon with a cool gaze. 'Take him away.'

The leprechauns around the demon adjusted the rings on their fingers and the black flame shrank as if stung. They marched their prisoner away.

Hurm Igrig surveyed the surrounding area. There were large fractures in the spirit realm. He shook his head as he looked at them. 'Operation White Flame complete,' he said to the remaining leprechauns. Then in a sighing, weary tone he added, 'Let's get started on the clean-up. This reality has taken quite a beating. *Hmmff.*'

CHAPTER SIXTEEN

OPERATION
WHITE FLAME

'What . . . what just happened?' Bethany asked as soon as there was some sense of normality. She joined Hurm Igrig by the collection of spirit mirrors. He was examining them in a way that was partly appreciation, partly disapproval.

'Quite something,' he muttered to himself. He registered Bethany and his lumpy, misshapen face broke into a genuine smile. 'Ah, Bethany, I must congratulate you. You did an outstanding job.'

She felt confused. 'I did?'

'Of course.' Hurm Igrig gestured to a pair of leprechauns in blue uniforms. They hurried over and he briefed them on reversing the magic of the mirrors. He turned to Bethany to give her his full attention. 'Now then,' he said. 'I think an explanation is in order.'

She took in the swarm of activity as lots of leprechauns filled the workshop. 'That would be nice,' she replied in a dazed tone.

The leprechaun nodded and took her gently by the arm. 'I'm afraid we had to make sure from the outset that you knew nothing about our intentions. I had grossly misjudged the power of the demon by the time it had stolen Quinn's identity. In truth, it took me a while to piece together what had happened. The demon had infiltrated our department and hidden its tracks. I was convinced that it not only posed no threat, but that it had been destroyed by you and Quinn at the hotel last year. I was foolish. If it hadn't been for Quinn's insistence in pursuing the case, I might have never suspected the truth.'

'You knew all along?' Bethany asked in amazement.

'It took me a while,' Hurm Igrig conceded. 'When Quinn stole the gold I began the investigation. It didn't take long for me to realise that it wasn't Quinn, particularly when he began to target you with curses. Do you remember the café where I first protected you?'

'I thought it was you that was cursing me.'

'My magic deflected the demon's curses. The demon manifested through the images of Quinn. You would have been crushed if I hadn't intervened with that first attack. And again when the demon struck outside the museum I managed to cause the car to avoid a direct collision with you. Only just. The demon was strong from the start.

That's why early on we came up with a plan.'

'What do you mean *we* came up with a plan?' She could see Pat, Seamus and Flannigan moving nearby, busily trying to defuse the curses that held Donovan captive in his mirror. They all happened to look over at that moment. They grinned and waved.

'Your friends,' Hurm Igrig said. 'Together we formed a plan not only to protect you, but also to use you as a way to break the demon's magic. You were the only one who could get near enough to Quinn to deliver the spell that could reverse the effects of the curse on him.'

'That ring?'

'That ring,' he confirmed. 'It contained the sacred white flame, the ancient magic we use to restore the balance. The white flame can undo any curse, reverse any spell.'

Bethany felt a flush of emotion – a mixture of anger and embarrassment that she hadn't noticed she had been tricked and manipulated. 'You used me.'

'We had to,' the leprechaun said gently, although unapologetically. 'We had to make sure that you delivered the ring directly to Quinn, and to do that we had to be certain that the demon believed the leprechauns had turned against you. Every other operative we sent in was stripped of their magic.' He nodded towards the mirrors. 'We knew the demon wanted to see you and Quinn utterly defeated. The demon had to believe that you didn't intend to be captured and imprisoned with Quinn but, more importantly, you had to believe that so that there was no hint of suspicion.'

'Are you saying *everything* was a set-up? The court case? The prison? All so I could end up getting that ring to Quinn?'

'The plan was twofold. Firstly, to protect you from the danger posed by the demon in the physical realm. Secondly, to use you to lull the demon into a false sense of security so that we could strike back.' Hurm Igrig fixed her with a solemn look. 'The court case was real, to some degree. The leprechauns certainly wanted justice. As I followed the demon's actions it became clear that it wanted revenge on you and Quinn. It was going to get that revenge by framing you both for a terrible crime that would result in your souls being removed. The demon pursued you into the physical realm and attacked you in the hope of hurting you so badly that it could capture you without a fight, then begin draining you as it had Quinn. I couldn't let that happen.'

'It was a set-up?' Bethany mumbled again, shell-shocked.

'The court case allowed us to keep you safely in the Stolen City. This also served as a way of making the demon think we had not seen through his deception. We even made sure that leprechauns were caught – Donovan included – that could corroborate this story to the demon. It was an extremely dangerous operation and I would not have conducted it if I didn't think you were strong enough, Bethany Chase. The demon was extremely powerful and that power was threatening to collapse this reality. You were the only one who could save Quinn. You said as much in that first meeting we had.'

Already, her thoughts were racing. The way it had all been orchestrated, the way it had all been carefully planned so that she would be made to look guilty, the damning trial, the convenient escape from jail, the constant distractions so that she forgot she was even wearing the ring. 'But how?' she asked, thinking of all the risks, all the dangers. 'How could you have known any of it would work?'

'Luck is one thing that we leprechauns are masters of. It is our strongest magic and we have learned how to use it to our advantage.'

'You used me,' she said again, flustered, upset. 'I didn't *do* anything! It was Flannigan and Pat and Seamus and Maggie-Maggie *and you* . . .'

'No,' Hurm Igrig said forcefully, so much so that it halted the tears that were prickling Bethany's eyes. 'No spirit could have done what you did. Flannigan may have told a few tall stories about you, but he was right in the main. You have a rare spirit.'

'But . . .'

'Our friends and our actions are more of our spirits than we care to realise, Bethany Chase. Remember that.' Hurm Igrig said this with such sincerity and tenderness that Bethany struggled to answer him. The leprechaun looked up from where they were standing. He pointed at the approaching figure. 'I think someone wants to thank you.'

Quinn appeared. The white flames that had smothered his body had now filtered back down to the ring on his hand. His spirit was clear and bright. As he strode up to Bethany his face broke open into a friendly grin. He grabbed her in a wide embrace and laughter poured out of him in a wonderful giggling stream of sound as he hugged her. All of Bethany's doubt, all of her embarrassment and anger dissolved away in that moment. She had helped her friend. It was as if a great weight had been lifted from her shoulders.

With this realisation came another, though, and Bethany broke free. 'My parents!' she shouted at the leprechauns. 'You made them unconscious. Are they OK? Are the cursed products still affecting them? We need to get them now. I need to get back to my body.'

Hurm Igrig made a calming gesture. 'Please, there is nothing to panic about. The situation is completely under control. They are fine.' He directed her attention to the workshop and the spells that the leprechauns were casting. The people who had previously been the Quinn clones were removing their masks, then falling to the floor in a swooning faint, a faint caused by the leprechauns. Other leprechauns were examining the Quinn products and removing the magic from them, collecting it in glowing pots.

'So, this looks organised,' Bethany commented. On the far wall, Flannigan, Seamus and Pat had released Donovan and were in the process of freeing Gurdo Erlstan.

'The clean-up operation will take some time,' Hurm Igrig noted, returning to his professional tone. 'We'll disable as much of the magic as we can and try to return things to normal as quickly as possible. Here, we're going to create an explosion that will act as a diversion from —'

'An explosion?!' Bethany shrieked.

Quinn laughed, a gurgling, spluttering noise.

'It will be completely safe, I assure you,' Hurm Igrig added. 'It will be found to have been caused by unstable chemical compounds used in the products. It will lead to the immediate withdrawal of all Quinn merchandise from shops. There will be investigations into the products that will reveal the use of toxic materials. That will lead to a public outcry and Quinn mania will die out quickly as a result. Quinn's remains – the Quinn the demon created – will be found at the scene of the explosion. This scene.'

'You've certainly thought this through,' Bethany murmured.

'Well, we leprechauns are devious spirits, after all,' Hurm Igrig said. 'It is in our nature.'

Bethany noticed how sad Quinn looked as he surveyed all the cursed products emblazoned with his face. 'It's OK. At least it's over now,' she reassured him.

He sighed and nodded.

'And that just leaves you, Bethany.' Hurm Igrig knitted his bushy eyebrows together in a serious frown. He led her forward, towards a table where she could make out the outline of her body. 'Your work in this operation has been exceptional. It has been noted by the Leprechaun High Council. We could use a spirit such as your good self to help in hunting demons. What do you say?'

Bethany wasn't sure what she was hearing. 'You want me to work for you?'

'In an official capacity, yes. As a demon hunter. But . . . it would mean you would become an inhabitant of the Stolen City. You would not be able to go back *there*.' He motioned to her physical body. He clicked his fingers, and the three of them rose up in a graceful gliding motion and landed on the table. They surveyed the sleeping face in front of them, large and still and without the healthy glow of a spirit. 'It is your choice. You can come with us, or you can stay. But I must warn you, if you stay you will not have any memory of what happened here. It is crucial that we remove any evidence of what really occurred. For you, that is all your recollections of the leprechauns, our city, Quinn and the demon, all your contact in the spirit realm. It will be quite extensive. Even your time in the Spellbound Hotel will have to be wiped. Do you understand?'

'That's a pretty big decision,' she replied, numb at the enormity of such a choice.

Hurm Igrig nodded. 'It is,' he agreed solemnly. 'It is.'

'But how can I . . .?' It all felt too much. So much had happened in such a short time. She needed time to think about things. She wanted to be back home with her parents, without a doubt, but there was something irresistible about the leprechauns, about their city and their strange existence. There was so much she wanted to discover, so many possibilities open to her, worlds that she could only begin to imagine. Yet she wanted a normal life, she *craved* a normal life. She wanted to make friends, to explore and experience *her* world.

In desperation, she found herself looking at Quinn for some sort of help. He didn't smile or laugh. His expression was one of calm, clear understanding, and it took Bethany a moment to realise why he was looking at her like that.

'It seems you have made your decision,' Hurm Igrig commented.

Confused, Bethany peered down at her spirit. It was beginning to drift towards her physical body. She could feel herself being dragged towards it, as if she was standing in a river with strong currents, pulling her along. 'Oh.'

The leprechauns were all turning to look at her. She could see Flannigan waving at her urgently, with Pat, Seamus and Donovan staring at her, their features caught in sad, resigned expressions. The entire room stopped. She could see faces staring at her respectfully. Some removed their hats. Some stood to attention.

Hurm Igrig bowed. 'Bethany Chase, it has been an honour.'

'I . . .' She felt herself slipping away. She waved one last time at Quinn. 'Thank you,' she managed to say before she was sucked down into the heavy, dense substance of her physical body.

The transition from one state to another was disorientating. Her thoughts swirled in a chaotic jumble. She wasn't sure what was real and what wasn't. She thought she glimpsed Maggie-Maggie leaning over her, smiling affectionately. 'We had to say goodbye, dearie,' left-headed Maggie said to her. 'And I'm afraid we'll have to take these back,' right-headed Maggie added. A ghostly hand reached down and removed the spirit glasses, like a cobweb being brushed away from her face. As the glasses were pulled free Bethany thought she caught sight of a flash of orange sparks connecting with her head and Hurm Igrig's lumpy, misshapen face. There was a sensation of her thoughts unravelling, rushing away from her.

Far away, an explosion rocked the foundations of a building. Walls shook, windows shattered, furniture toppled.

'Good work. Time to go,' said a voice.

CHAPTER SEVENTEEN

GOING HOME

Bethany was aware that she was in an ambulance. She woke as if from a long and deep sleep, and had an inexplicable feeling of relief, although she had no idea why she should feel that way. Her thoughts were jumbled and muggy.

A female paramedic with a friendly face looked down at her. 'She's awake,' she announced. Two figures jumped up behind her and hurried over.

'Bethany!' her father exclaimed.

'Oh, Bethany, you're OK,' her mother cried with relief.

'Mum? Dad?'

Her parents looked a state. They were dishevelled, covered in dust and wrapped in blankets to keep them warm. By the looks of them they must have been to a fancy-dress party as they had colourful make-up dripping down their faces in gooey streaks and dyed pink hair that straggled over their brows. 'Everything's going to be fine,' Mrs Chase told her.

The paramedic carried out a quick series of tests, then patted Bethany on the shoulder. 'The good news is, you seem to be in working order. We're taking you all to hospital as a precaution, but it's nothing to be worried about.'

Groggily, Bethany asked, 'What happened?'

Her parents seemed as confused and vague as Bethany felt. 'Ummm, well, we're trying to piece that together ourselves. There was the winning ticket . . .' Mrs Chase said.

'And I think we met Quinn,' Mr Chase added uncertainly.

Mrs Chase nodded in agreement. 'I definitely remember stepping into the lobby of his house.'

'Then it gets a bit . . . blurry.' Mr Chase looked at Bethany. 'How much do you remember?'

She concentrated and tried to recall the last thing that had happened to her. 'Are we in London?' she said uncertainly.

Her parents exchanged worried glances.

'And who is Quinn?' she asked. She examined her parents. 'And what *are* you wearing?'

Nurses checked with doctors who checked with consultants who checked with specialists. Bethany and her parents had to sit through a series of tests, then scans, then examinations, which involved a lot of waiting around. They watched the television reports as they moved from one department of the hospital to another, fascinated that they had been involved in such a huge news story. Helicopter images showed a row of houses with its windows blown out. Each reporter sounded more dramatic than the last.

'. . . at the site of Quinn's personal residence. These classical three-storey properties in the heart of Mayfair were the scene of a shocking explosion at two o'clock this afternoon. Initial reports suggest that highly volatile chemicals have been found on the premises used in the manufacture of Quinn products. Nobody was hurt in the explosion, but property was damaged and over twenty staff members are in hospital as a result. Police are not . . .'

On another channel they saw pictures of fire-fighters checking the remains of a charred room full of Quinn merchandise.

'. . . bizarre rumours of cats seen entering the house before the explosion were unconfirmed. What is certain is that officials are viewing this incident very seriously. Several factories involved in the production of Quinn merchandise have already been raided . . .'

Bethany and her parents baulked at the last clip they saw, showing Mr and Mrs Chase being helped into the back of the ambulance containing Bethany. It was strange seeing themselves on television and they all laughed nervously at the sight of themselves.

'. . . this poor family had no idea what had happened to them. Only hours before they had been winners of a much hyped competition. Now, that dream has become a nightmare.'

'Great. My fifteen minutes of fame and I look a mess,' Mrs Chase complained.

Mr Chase chuckled quietly to himself. 'I don't know, I thought you were very dignified,' he joked.

A nurse interrupted them, showing them through to the neurologist's office. A jovial man with a short scruffy beard was examining several print-outs as they sat down in front of his desk.

'Well, I've had a look over the results and I'm glad to say there's no cause for concern,' he said in a cheery manner. He addressed Mr and Mrs Chase. 'Your memory loss doesn't seem significant. I was a little more concerned about your daughter. I can't adequately explain why her amnesia spans so many weeks but . . .' He sighed and smiled at Bethany. 'Your functions are fine. Nothing has turned up on the scans. No blurring, no slurring, no aches or pains. It may pass, it may not. Either way, it doesn't seem to have affected you in any other way. Do you feel OK?'

Bethany nodded.

'Then that's all that matters,' he said with a conclusive nod. He showed them out of his office, telling them to come back if there were any problems, and they felt a sense of relief as they wandered through the long hospital corridors.

As they made it to the exit a loud woman's voice called out. '*There* you are. I can't tell you how worried I was. I knew something bad was going to happen.' Aunt Bess ran over to meet them. 'Have you seen the news?' She kissed each of them on the cheek and guided them towards a nearby taxi. 'It has been an eventful few days.'

'Agreed,' Mrs Chase sighed in an exhausted tone.

'Eventful is not the word,' Mr Chase groaned.

Bethany stared out the window of the taxi all the way back to Aunt Bess's house. Everywhere she looked she could see evidence of Quinn and his curious products. She didn't know who he was, but it looked as though he must have been very popular. That popularity seemed to be vanishing, though. She could see his posters being taken down from shop windows and his products being removed from shelves. This might not have been so strange if Bethany hadn't noticed so many cats near the shops, staring inquisitively at the Quinn products – not very well cats by the look of them, as they seemed to be sneezing an awful lot.

As the taxi pulled up by a set of lights she peeked out of the window and saw someone standing by the car reading a magazine. The picture on the front of the magazine was of Quinn, and for the briefest moment Bethany had a strange sense of déjà vu.

'You OK?' her mum asked.

'Yeah, fine,' Bethany said. When she looked back out the person holding the magazine had disappeared and the déjà vu evaporated. 'Mum,' Bethany whispered. 'Are we going home?'

'Well, we're going back to your aunt's house. Do you remember that?' her mother asked. 'With all the cats and dogs?'

Bethany shook her head. 'No, not really.'

Mrs Chase's brow furrowed with concern.

'You know, you can stay as long as you want,' Aunt Bess said. 'If it will help. You've been through a lot.'

Mr Chase cleared his throat and turned to her. 'Listen, sis, you've been so kind and that's a generous offer but . . . I think we need to get home. Maybe London's not the place for us after all. We're going to make a go of it in Stagtree Knoll, even if that means being hard up for a little while.'

A brief look of understanding passed over Aunt Bess's face. She nodded. 'Of course,' she said. 'You must do what feels right.'

Nobody spoke for several minutes.

The four of them viewed the busy London streets. The shops were beginning to close. People were rushing home from their jobs and there was a weary atmosphere to the city. It was the last day of the summer holidays, but Bethany felt full of hope and excitement at the thought of returning home. The year ahead was full of wonderful possibilities, she was sure. There were friendships to be made, places to explore, and, most importantly, fun to be had.

Yes, Bethany thought. *It feels right.*

DARE
YOU
ENTER?

thespellboundhotel.com

Find out how Bethany first met Quinn!

TOM EGLINGTON

Strange things are going on in the village of Stagtree Knoll. Ever since Bethany's parents moved here they have developed an unhealthy obsession for the local sausages. Not to mention the bizarre soap opera they watch every night without fail, a soap opera that seems to have hypnotised everyone in the village. Everyone apart from Bethany, that is.

Determined to find out what is going on, she sneaks into the mysterious Stoames mansion and discovers something very strange indeed – a hotel for ghosts, spirits and non-material beings.

But Bethany is not a welcome guest here and if she hopes to escape and save her parents, she must face the sinister power at the heart of the hotel, and break the spell it has cast over everyone.

☆

www.piccadillypress.co.uk

Go online to discover:

☆ more books you'll love

☆ competitions

☆ chapter downloads

☆ author interviews

☆ fun quizzes

☆ and much more!